Home Sweet Home

A SWEET, TEXAS NOVELLA

By Candis Terry

SWEET SURPRISE
SOMETHING SWEETER
SWEETEST MISTAKE
ANYTHING BUT SWEET
SOMEBODY LIKE YOU
ANY GIVEN CHRISTMAS
SECOND CHANCE AT THE SUGAR SHACK

Coming Soon
TRULY SWEET

Short Stories
SWEET COWBOY CHRISTMAS
SWEET FORTUNE (appears in
CONFESSIONS OF A SECRET ADMIRER)

Home Sweet Home

A Sweet, Texas Novella

CANDIS TERRY

AVONIMPULSE
An Imprint of HarperCollinsPublishers

Home Sweet

Home

"Home Sweet Home" was originally published in an altered form in the e-book anthology *For Love and Honor* in June 2012 by Avon Impulse, an Imprint of HarperCollins Publishers.

Excerpt from *Truly Sweet* copyright © 2015 by Candis Terry.

EPub Edition MAY 2015 ISBN: 9780062420893
Print Edition ISBN: 9780062423238

10 9 8 7 6 5 4 3 2 1

Author's Note

Dear Reader,

When I first wrote "Home Sweet Home," it was just the beginning of my adventures in Sweet, Texas. At the time, I was unfamiliar with the Wilder family, a crazy fashionista goat, an octogenarian cowboy Casanova, and an entire cast of lovable characters that eventually came with the series. Once in a lifetime you get lucky and you get a do-over. I was thrilled to have the opportunity to go back and take a deeper look at former U.S. Army Ranger Lieutenant Aiden Marshall and Paige Walker's story.

Aiden has always been a courageous, confident man of action, but the deaths of his two best friends and having to leave his beloved four-legged friend back in Afghanistan have shaken him to the core. Paige Walker has loved Aiden all her life, and she's anxiously waited for him to return home. When he finally arrives, he's not quite the man she'd known before he left. Now it's her turn to be courageous. And very, very patient.

I hope you'll enjoy this extended version of Aiden and Paige's story. It was so nice to get to revisit them, and Sweet, Texas, and fall in love all over again. In Rennie's honor, a portion of the proceeds for this novella will go to several animal rescues, including a few here in my own hometown.

I love to connect with my readers, so be sure to pop by my Web site www.candisterry.com for all the latest happenings.

Happy reading!
Candis Terry

This is dedicated to the men, women, and families of the Idaho Army National Guard at Gowen Field and the Mountain Home Air Force Base. Please accept my heartfelt thanks for your service and dedication. You keep us safe. You make us proud. God bless.

Chapter One

WHEN YOU GREW up in a town the size of a flea circus, anonymity was impossible.

There hadn't been a chance in hell he could have slipped back in unnoticed even if being elusive had been a part of his profession and survival.

As an Army Ranger, Lieutenant Aiden Marshall had been to some of the most hellish corners on earth, and no one had been the wiser. Except for maybe the enemy. Yet the moment he'd cranked the key in the ignition of his old pickup, it seemed the entire population of Sweet, Texas, had heard the engine catch.

Today, he'd traded his fatigues for an old T-shirt and Levi's, but the dog tags pressed against his heart verified he'd be a soldier till the day they put him in the ground.

He was damned lucky he wasn't there already.

As he drove the winding road through pastures where longhorns grazed and clusters of prickly pear cactus shot up amid the tall grass, he did not take for granted the faded yellow ribbons hugging the thick trunks of the tall oaks that bordered the road. Those ribbons had been placed there for all the men and women who served. That selected group included him and two of his best child-hood friends. All three of them had enlisted the same day. Survived boot camp and Ranger training together. Hit the sands of Afghanistan as one. Fought side by side.

He'd been the only one to make it back home.

The lucky one, everyone said.

He wasn't so sure he shared the sentiment.

In the trenches, he and his buddies had added one more friend to their unit. One more who'd proven faith-ful, devoted, and trustworthy. One who'd offered com-fort on long, dark nights and lonely days.

One more Aiden had been forced to leave behind.

The pressure in his chest tightened as he lifted his hand in a wave to the group of seniors in jogging shoes who waited to cross the road. On the way to his destina-tion, he could not ignore the joy on the faces of those who waved or shouted "welcome back" as he passed by.

Those in his community knew none of the lingering an-guish that kept him awake night after night. They were just happy he'd made it home. In one piece was an added plus.

Too bad he felt anything but whole.

His hometown had been hit hard by the loss of sev-eral upstanding soldiers. Men he'd been honored to serve with. As a survivor, he felt none of the joy and all of the guilt. Harder than strapping on his weapons and facing the enemy were the visits he'd paid to those heroes' families upon his return. Looking them in the eye and expressing his sorrow for their loss, admitting he'd been unable to save his friends—their loved ones—had been devastating.

He should have seen it coming.

Should have been able to detect the IED that had blown up beneath their feet.

But he hadn't.

And they'd died.

Over and over, Aiden wished he could trade places with them.

But he could not.

All he could do was offer an apology and his condolences to their loved ones. In his mind, that was too little, too late. Inadequate. Absurd. Yet it did not surprise him that these kind people took him into their embrace and offered him consolation he did not deserve. After all, they'd raised great men who'd given their lives for their country. Still, the losses—the memories—emotionally ripped the heart from his chest and the breath from his lungs.

Surviving was not all it was cracked up to be.

He had nothing left to give. To anyone. But that didn't make the reason for his current destination any easier.

Not at all.

On Main Street, beneath the old water tower where local businesses displayed patriotic signs and the flagpole in Town Square flew a pristine Stars and Stripes, Aiden eased his truck into the gravel lot beside Bud's Nothing Finer Diner.

Over the years, the good people of Sweet had tried their best to make the town appeal to tourists. The apple orchards—like the one his family owned—had blossomed into bed-and-breakfasts, art galleries, antique shops, and wine rooms. Judging by the near-empty streets, the place still had a long way to go.

In a space near the diner's front door, he cut the truck's engine, leaned back in the seat, and inhaled the aroma of thick, juicy burgers and sweet-potato fries that floated in through the window on the warm summer breeze.

Nostalgia clogged his throat and made him wish he could reverse time. Like Marty McFly, he wished he could go back to the future and change the course of events. But everyone knew wishes were a waste of time, and reality often ruled with a heavy hand.

Bud's Diner was little more than a yellow concrete box, but since the day Aiden had been old enough to sit at the counter, he'd enjoyed the extra thick milk shakes and homemade eats that made his mouth water. Even when he'd been halfway across the world, he'd craved that tasty connection to the place he loved.

Bud's was the first place the townsfolk came together to mourn, celebrate, or discuss local politics. It was a gathering spot for the elders to play checkers and the younger set to go on a date. Within its red vinyl booths, there had been proposals of marriage, reconciliations, and rumor had it that in 1964, Betty Jean Crawford had gone into labor and had nearly given birth because she wouldn't go to the hospital until she finished her Diablo burger and chocolate milk shake.

Today, all bets were off. Aiden had an unpleasant task ahead of him. Regret burned like a bonfire in his chest as he snatched the keys from the ignition and stepped out of his truck.

Through six tours and countless missions in the Middle East, his mouth had watered for a slice of home. He was about to ease his craving.

Even if he had to wash it down with a sour note.

The bell above the door announced his arrival to the ranchers and community members who huddled inside around tables nicked and scarred by years of diners with eager appetites. Marv Woodrow, a World War II vet, stood on feeble legs and gave him a salute. Bill McBride, a Vietnam vet, stood and gave him a one-armed hug and a fist bump. The rest also welcomed him home as he made his way toward the busy counter. Graciously, he accepted their warm welcome though the soldier and man of lost friends inside him rebelled.

Why he was still here when his friends were not was a part of the puzzle that would never fit.

He glanced around the diner at the wood-paneled walls and the Don't Mess with Texas décor. As wonderful as the greetings had been, there was one person he'd looked forward to seeing the most. Even though he wouldn't enjoy giving her the news he had to deliver.

Back in the kitchen, a good-natured argument surfaced.

"Pick up your own danged pickles, Bud. I've got my hands full of Arlene's sweet-potato fries, a Diablo burger for Curtis, and Walter's patty melt."

"But the pickles are burnin' in the fryer, girl."

A feminine sigh of exasperation lifted above the lunchtime chatter and forks clanging on plates. At the sound, the pressure in Aiden's chest tightened even as a rare smile pushed at the corners of his mouth.

Before he could breathe, the owner of that sassy tone marched out of the kitchen with her thick, honey-colored ponytail swinging in rhythm with the sway of her hips.

"Here's your melt, Walter." She set an overflowing plate down in front of the old guy at the end of the counter. "Don't be surprised if that hunk of meat finds its way back to the cow before Bud gets movin' back there."

Aiden picked up the plastic-coated menu he could recite blindfolded and watched her work. Quick hands and a sweet smile despite the snap in her words. A pair of jeans hugged her slender thighs and a yellow Bud's Diner T-shirt molded to her full breasts and small waist.

A flurry of memories rushed back. Memories of sweet kisses, hot sex, and the delectable scent of her warm, sun-kissed skin. Good thing he was sitting down. Just looking at her while she swiped a towel over the counter had his lower half standing at attention.

Catching a glimpse of a new customer from the corner of her eye, she drawled, "I'll be right with ya, darlin'." Two seconds later, she tossed the towel in an out-of-sight workspace, pulled her order pad from the pocket of her apron, and made her way toward his end of the counter.

"What can I . . ." Pencil poised, her blue eyes lifted, and that beautiful, plump mouth slid into a warm smile. "You're back," she said in a slow whisper.

A quick heartbeat passed while her gaze ate him up.

Before he could blink, she launched herself into his arms.

FROM THE MOMENT she'd figured out the difference between boys and girls, Paige Walker had known what she wanted in life.

And what she wanted was Aiden Marshall.

He'd been a rough-and-tumble boy who'd cleverly escaped her amorous elementary-school intentions when she'd tried to talk him into kissing her behind the cafeteria. She'd finally caught him in high school, where *he* became the scholar and *she* the willing student in their kissing lessons. He'd been her first love and the only man she'd ever let into her heart or her body. Together, they'd learned how to love, disagree, and how to kiss and make up. They'd whispered promises in the dark and made things happen during the day.

They'd been together almost every day until the darkest day in America crashed down in the nightmare no one had ever expected. The following week, Aiden, Billy Marks, and Bobby Hansen enlisted in the Army.

After that, everything changed.

When Aiden had left for boot camp, he made her no promises and warned her he wasn't much of a letter writer. Once he'd been approved for Ranger training, his previously infrequent letters dwindled. And over the past couple of years, he'd barely sent more than a quick note or two. Though he'd told her not to, she'd promised him that she would wait.

And she had.

Now, as his strong arms curled around her and tucked her in close, she knew all those lonely nights she'd waited with worry and fear burrowed into her heart had been worth every second.

Aiden was home.

Safe.

Sound.

Home.

Paige pressed her cheek against his faded T-shirt and listened to the steady heartbeat in his chest. She inhaled the fresh scent of his soap and his underlying masculine heat. With a sigh, she leaned her head back and looked up at him while her fingers molded around his hard, defined biceps.

A man like Aiden was impossible to ignore unless you had severely poor eyesight, or you just didn't care for a guy with a movie-star face and a body honed for elite military missions. On top of all that, he had the most amazing mouth—soft, manly lips that knew how to give a girl a kiss she'd remember until one day—years later— she could kiss him again.

Today, he'd discarded his army fatigues and settled into a worn pair of Levi's that accented his long, muscular legs and cupped his generous package like a lover's hand. He looked so good, she wanted to lay him down on the counter and feast on him like an all-you-can-eat Sunday buffet.

On a good day, Aiden's short dark hair and the spark in his brown eyes could stun the breath in her lungs.

Today, the power of that impact doubled. She hadn't seen him in over two years—when last he'd come home to his dying father's bedside.

Since then, all hell had broken loose, and Aiden had stood beneath the deluge of destruction.

Today, while he stood close enough for her to touch and hold, Paige knew in her heart that Aiden Marshall was a changed man.

While she told herself it only mattered that he was safe, and everything would be just fine, her fears resurfaced.

Aiden might be home.

But the smile in his eyes had vanished.

Chapter Two

"WHEN DID YOU get home? Why didn't your brother tell me? How long will you be home? Do you want something to eat? Of course you do. Dumb question. Scratch that."

Aiden couldn't help but smile as Paige fired off a volley of questions, then finished them off with a random thought.

Just like old times.

She'd always been that girl.

The one who had a million things going on all at once and tried to keep them all in order inside her head. At times, she came off a bit scrambled even though, for the most part, she had it more together than anyone he'd ever met. Aiden knew she saw every day as a gift. She saw life as something priceless that should be hit at full speed and explored twenty-four hours a day.

When they'd been together, he'd managed to keep her in bed for several of those hours a day just to show her that a lot could be accomplished in a prone position too. But even then, between making love, she'd come up with a list of half a dozen things she wanted to do that day, next week, or a year down the road. They'd done a hell of a lot of exploring in those days, and even if he hadn't been able to keep up with her eagerness on the calendar, he managed to keep her enthusiasm busy in other ways.

"A few days ago," he said, answering her first question, then followed up with the rest. "Ben didn't tell you because he didn't know. And yes, I'd love a Diablo burger, a double order of sweet-potato fries, and a marshmallow Snickers milk shake."

It didn't take a rocket scientist to know immediately that she was hurt because he'd taken so long to come see her. By rights, she should have been first on his list. And she would have been, but he had obligations to visit Bobby's and Billy's folks. And after those visits, he had barely been able to look at himself in the mirror.

The wounded look in her eye disappeared, and her smile reappeared. Apparently, she realized too why he hadn't come to see her first.

"Awww. Your favorite foods." She shifted her weight from one sexy hip to the other. "I'll bet you've been craving those for a long time."

He'd been craving her too, but that kind of thinking had to stop.

"Pretty much since I boarded the plane for Afghanistan and left American soil." Funny how the moment you knew you couldn't have something, you wanted it even more.

"Well, the wait is over. You sit right there, and I'll have Bud put your order on a rail." Her tennis shoes squeaked as she turned and rushed off into the kitchen.

With all day in front of him and nothing to do, Aiden watched her through the order window, excitedly gesturing with her hands while she spoke with Bud. Still, he couldn't help wonder out loud . . . "A rail?"

The old man with the bald head next to him nodded and grinned. "She's puttin' the *hurry up* on it for you."

"Oh."

Guilt wrapped around Aiden's throat and gave a hard squeeze. The faster Paige moved, the sooner he'd have to deliver the news. She looked so damned happy to see him, he hated to burst her bubble. Hated to hurt her in any way. But it had to be done. No matter how badly he might think he wanted it to be otherwise.

"For a man who's got a pretty woman like that scurrying around to make time to be with him, you sure got a grim look on your puss."

The man sitting next to him, Chester Banks, was well into his eighties. He'd had more ex-wives than Disneyland had rides. Over the years, his nose had grown, and his eyes had sunk. He probably weighed all of a hundred pounds soaking wet, was bowlegged, and wore his Wranglers so starched, his arthritic knees could barely bend. But Chester had no qualms whatsoever about chasing the ladies who were at least six decades younger.

"Probably matches what's inside my head," Aiden verified.

"Oh?" A scraggly gray brow lifted, and a smile broke across Chester's wrinkled lips. "So you're saying the lovely Paige is up for grabs?"

"That would be up to her." Aiden chuckled. "Although I have to warn you that if she takes offense to your grabbing, she's got a hell of a right hook."

"No worries." Chester gave a confident nod and a wink. "I got the gift."

"Care to let us fledglings in on *the gift*?"

"Ain't giving my secrets away. Don't need the competition." Chester sipped his coffee and grinned like he alone held the key to Fort Knox. "Those Wilder brothers give me enough trouble as it is. Don't need the added pressure from the likes of you."

"Not even a hint?"

"Okay. Maybe just one." The old man sighed. "Ya got to sweet-talk 'em. Make all them pretty promises they want to hear."

"That's the secret?"

"Yep. One of 'em. Use that, and I guarantee they'll drop their lacy underthings faster than you can say yippee-ki-yay."

Aiden sipped the water Paige had set down in front of him so he didn't bark out a laugh at Chester's excessive confidence. Trouble was, even though he might want to sweet-talk the lovely Paige out of her lacy underthings, that's not what he'd come here to do. And that blew higher than any mortar he'd ever seen hit the sands of Afghanistan.

AFTER SEVERAL HOURS of hearty conversation with those who lingered at Bud's Diner long after the lunch crowd had dispersed and a warm slice of apple crumb pie à la mode, Aiden and his full stomach leaned back in the chair. On a normal day, he would have taken off as soon as he was done eating. Instead, while he waited for Paige to finish up her shift, he listened intently to Hazel and Ray Calhoun excitedly describe how the senior center had contacted a new TV makeover show to put a fresh face on their small town to increase tourism.

Aiden couldn't imagine why Hollywood would ever come this far south. It only mattered that the folks in this town and other small towns across America cared enough to try to make things better. These hardworking, generous-hearted people were the reason he, Billy, and Bobby had enlisted.

In the midst of Hazel's describing the TV show's designer host, a dainty hand with clean, short nails settled over his shoulder. He looked up into the blue eyes he'd dreamed of on many a lonely night, and a sudden jolt struck him hard in the center of his chest.

Paige had always had a way of doing that to him.

Even now, when he knew the heart had been ripped out of him, and he had nothing left to give.

"If y'all are done monopolizing the lieutenant's time," Paige said in a teasing drawl, "I'd like to borrow him for a bit."

"Oh pooh." Gertie West wrinkled up her nose. "We were just getting to the good stuff."

Aiden glanced out the front window, where the sun hung low in the sky. As much as he'd like to, he couldn't put off the conversation he and Paige needed to have any longer. It would be unfair to her and selfish of him.

"My apologies." He stood and pushed the chair back. "I really do need to get going."

"You come back tomorrow, young man, and we'll buy you another slice of that apple pie," Ray Calhoun said. "We want to hear all about your adventures."

Adventures.

Not exactly what he'd call them. Wasn't likely he'd discuss them either. Especially when he was trying so hard to forget them. He gave the afternoon diners at the table a nod and turned toward Paige.

"Come with me." She smiled wide enough to flash her pretty white teeth. "I have something I want to show you."

"Your car or mine?"

She slipped her hand into his and tugged him toward the door. "How about, for old time's sake, we take your truck?"

The warmth of her palm sent a tingle down into his chest, and a sensual flood of memories he thought he'd buried long ago popped up fresh like a spring daisy.

"Sun's still shining." Thinking back to all those hot summer nights they'd drove his truck out into the hills and he'd reveled in Paige's youthful abandon, he smiled and gave her hand a squeeze. "I think the population of Sweet might take offense to your whipping off that T-shirt for old time's sake."

"Wouldn't be my first offense." Her grin told him she was thinking about those crazy summer nights a long time ago when she had let go of her inhibitions and he'd been right there to appreciate the loss. "Come on. We're wasting daylight."

As she tugged him through the gravel parking lot, he watched the way her hips swayed. Nothing outrageously obvious. Just a smooth motion that belied the passion lit deep in her core.

He'd almost forgotten all the little idiosyncrasies she possessed. Like the way she lifted her arms toward the moon when she was on top of him, giving him the best sex of his life. Or the way she'd snuggle right against his side and drape her smooth leg over his hips. Or even the way she'd reach for him in her sleep, then sigh when she found him.

He'd carried those memories with him through boot camp. Through extensive Ranger training. Through numerous deployments to Iraq and Afghanistan.

Then, one day, everything around him exploded.

Normal existence had stopped.

And the memories perished.

After that, he hadn't allowed himself to think of the things that had made him happy. He didn't deserve to be happy. Not when those closest to him—those he was supposed to protect—were no longer able to have happy thoughts.

Without hesitation, Paige climbed up into his truck and slid right to the middle, where she'd always sat.

When he moved onto the seat beside her, she grinned like someone had just handed her a present. His hand paused on the key in the ignition.

How the hell could he even consider breaking her heart?

He didn't want to.

But for her own good, it had to be done.

Chapter Three

PAIGE TRIED TO remain positive though Aiden's smile had once again disappeared. She knew the hell he'd been through from the stories his brother Ben had relayed. She knew losing his two best friends had forever changed him. Those three boys had been attached at the hip since elementary school. They'd busted cows, busted heads, and busted a few bones together in the course of becoming men. And all the while, she had admired them for their loyalty to each other.

The war had changed things.

Time had passed and become like a long, desolate stretch of road between her and Aiden. She couldn't expect they'd just pick up where they'd left off—even though that was her wish. From the moment she'd heard the news that his duty had been served, and he intended to leave the military, she'd made a vow that no matter what, she'd keep a smile on her face.

For both of them.

She didn't know what he had planned moving forward, but she'd see him through whatever demons he had to face. Because no matter how much time had passed or what tragedies had occurred, there had never been a doubt that she loved him with her whole heart.

And nothing could ever take that away.

While Keith Urban sang about days going by, she leaned forward and turned up the radio. "Hang a right on Dandelion Street."

Aiden turned his head and looked at her with those deep brown eyes that made her think of the many wonderful nights she'd spent with him looking down at her while their bodies spoke the oldest language in the universe. "You moved?"

She nodded as the truck rambled down her street. "A little over a year ago."

"You still have Cricket?" he asked of the border collie mix she'd rescued from the shelter.

"Of course. She's still got a good amount of crazy going on, but age seems to have settled her down a bit."

"Happens to the best of us, I guess."

"Pull in there." She pointed toward the long gravel driveway that invited visitors up to a gingerbread Victorian that sat behind a white picket fence. Lately, she'd been doing research on restoring the painted lady to its former grandeur. Unfortunately, the amount of work to be done stole her breath. Even if she worked day and night, she might never get it all done by herself.

Aiden ducked his head to get a better look through the windshield. "Isn't this your aunt Bertie's place?"

"Was." She reached down and grabbed her purse from the floorboard. "Aunt Bertie developed dementia, and we had to put her in assisted care. She needed the money, so I bought the place. Come on. I'll show you around."

"You bought *this*?" He got out of the truck and looked up at the large two-story house. "On a waitress's salary?"

"Shocking isn't it?" While he stood there gawking, she walked around the front of the truck, took his hand, and led him toward the front door.

"Actually," she said, "I bought it on the salary I make at Bud's, plus the money I make doing taxes and accounting for a few local businesses. I make money from the apple orchard too."

"Taxes?"

"Oooh." She laughed at the sudden wrinkle between his eyes. "You look so surprised. I like that."

"Definitely surprised. I remember your skipping out on geometry class more than once because you never liked math."

"That was before I realized its benefits." She turned the key in the lock and pushed the door open. "I completed my bachelor's via the Internet," she explained. "I'm now the proud owner of a business administration degree. Got a gold tassel and everything."

"You've been busy." He stepped inside the foyer, gave a slow whistle, and rocked back on the heels of his worn cowboy boots. "You're a very impressive woman, Paige Walker."

"I know." The praise made her smile. "But you'd better be careful because I have a whole bunch of *impressive* locked away that's just been waiting to be unleashed."

A glimmer lit up his eyes, and hope warmed in her heart.

He didn't need to ask what she meant. He'd seen her *impressive* side before. Hopefully, he'd want to see it again.

She reached out, took his hand, and gave him the nickel tour of Honey Hill—named after the honeycrisp apples that grew in the orchard back between the barn and the creek.

The place was way more than she needed right now. But she had big plans. Always the optimist, she'd purchased the oversized home. With *him* in mind. But she'd wait to drop that little surprise. The man was edgy enough. No need to make him put on his running shoes.

"Looks like neither you nor your sister mind putting in a lot of hard work," he said.

"Oh . . . you know. A girl's got to have something to do to keep her out of trouble. Actually, Faith is the one who talked me into buying it. And not only to help out a relative." Paige led him through the dining room and into the kitchen. "Over a bottle of chardonnay, she started tossing out ideas that sounded reasonable and appealing."

She chuckled. "That's probably the last time I'll listen to her when she's been tipping a wineglass."

"What's your sister up to these days?"

"She's back home in Sweet now. Gave up the medical career to become an entrepreneur. When our uncle Charles passed, he left his property to Faith. Since then, she's put in a ton of work and turned that run-down cattle ranch into a guest ranch. She's got it operating almost full-time now, with a pool, hot tub, and guesthouses."

"That *is* ambitious."

"I know. I hardly see her anymore. But she loves it. So she decided I should have the same love affair with Honey Hill." She opened the refrigerator door. "Beer or sweet tea?"

The look he passed her way her gave Paige the feeling he'd run, given the chance.

Why, she wasn't certain. She'd tried to be careful with what she said, and he should know by now she was the last person he needed to be cautious with. But from the moment he'd walked through the door at Bud's, a look of hesitation had shadowed his eyes.

Maybe he was still tired from the trip home. Or all the troubles poking at his brain. Or the weight of the losses he'd suffered. Maybe all he really needed was to sit back and relax a little. Kick his feet up and unwind. Or maybe all he really needed was a few hot hours between the sheets. Whatever he needed, she'd be happy to provide.

"I shouldn't have either." He glanced at the door. "I should . . . probably go."

"Nonsense. You just got here." Because he suddenly appeared even more uneasy, she made the decision for him. Reaching into the refrigerator, she grabbed a bottle of Shiner Bock Ale, popped the cap, and smiled as their fingers met over the cold amber glass as she handed him the bottle. "Besides, you look like you could use a friend. You hungry?"

"After everything I ate at Bud's, I shouldn't think about eating for a week."

"But you've always had a healthy appetite."

"You get used to eating less when you're in the military. And you learn to eat fast before some hungry guy snatches away your plate. Bobby used to do that all the time." A wobbly smile tilted his lips, and a low chuckle rumbled in his chest. "He'd point and say something stupid like, 'Look, there's Mickey Mouse,' and I'd fall for it every time. Next thing I knew, I'd be picking the crumbs from my plate so I didn't starve."

He took a sip from the bottle, and Paige watched his throat work as he swallowed. She hoped in time he'd be able to remember the good times more. She hoped he'd think of his friends and be able to smile without its hurting so much. But she figured those days were a long way off. Right now, maybe being able to relax a little might be just the medicine he needed.

When it came to Aiden, she'd give her all. Her best. Hopefully, in the end, he'd realize that she'd waited a very long time for him for a reason.

They belonged together.

No matter what life threw in their paths, they could make it through as long as they had each other.

LATER, ON THE back veranda, Aiden lifted a chilled bottle of Shiner to his lips and drank. The beer tasted crisp and smooth. He hadn't been treated to a home-state brew in a long time and was enjoying every single ounce. Paige's gigantic backyard offered a phenomenal view of a lush landscape accented by rows and rows of apple trees laden with ripening fruit.

Curled up at his feet lay Cricket, Paige's brown-and-black border collie. While Paige had gone inside to throw together a meal for them to share, he and Cricket had played fetch with a slobbered-up tennis ball.

A heaving sigh now lifted the dog's broad chest. Apparently, he'd worn her out, as her breathing had become deep and even. Not a single brown eyebrow or white paw even twitched.

On impulse, he reached down and combed his fingers through her soft fur. When she looked up at him with those deep brown trusting eyes, a fist grabbed hold of his heart and squeezed.

He'd always thought of himself as a man who could handle anything. But lately, his losses refused to lessen their grip on his conscience. And that kept his heart in a constant state of misery.

"Need a refill?" Paige came toward the wrought-iron patio set where he sat. Her hands balanced plates of plump, juicy pieces of barbecued chicken and a mountainous portion of potato salad.

"Thanks." He lifted the bottle. "I'm good."

She set the plates down, and the aroma wafted up and tickled his appetite. "I don't suppose there were many beers to be found in the Middle East."

"Not really. Lots of sand to chew on, though."

She flashed a quick smile as she sat down opposite him and handed him a fork and knife. Earlier at Bud's, he'd delved into a juicy Diablo burger and apple pie so sweet it zinged his teeth. Yet as the tangy honey flavor of Paige's barbecue rolled across his tongue, he felt like a starving man.

"Good thing I cooked last night." She sipped from her wineglass. "Or this would be carrot sticks and Goldfish crackers."

"Didn't you used to eat those all the time in high school?"

"Yep. They even make them in rainbow colors now." She grinned. "You can have a different color for every meal."

He laughed. "Only *you* could make a feast out of a baked cracker."

"I can make a meal out of chocolate chip cookies too. Speaking of, did you get the packages I sent?"

"Yes. Thank you. I shared. Your oatmeal raisin cookies and the teriyaki jerky went over the best with the boys."

She took a bite of chicken, then looked up with a glimmer of mischief in her blue eyes. "Good thing I checked the guidelines before I sent those girly magazines."

"Yeah, totally against the rules." He chuckled. "But definitely would have been appreciated. Especially when everything you see over there is camo or brown."

"Brown?"

"Brown dirt. Brown sky. Brown sand. Brown structures."

"Ah. Sounds lovely." She reached across the table and snagged a chicken leg from the enormous portion on his plate.

"Hey. No fair stealing."

A grin flashed just before her teeth sank into the meat and tore off a chunk.

"You think you can just pick up where you left off with swiping my food? You didn't even wait this time till I wasn't looking."

"You never minded sharing, and you know it."

She was right. Unlike other girls, Paige had never been shy about taking what she wanted. She'd never been shy about eating in front of him. She'd never been shy about snatching a fry from his plate or even a bite of his cheeseburger.

To his delight, on many occasions over the years, she had, in fact, turned eating into an erotic adventure. And he hadn't minded that at all.

Her tongue darted out to lick away a smear of sauce from her top lip, and his body went on full alert. During his deployments, he'd fantasized about Paige. Her passion. The softness of her skin. The firmness of her breasts beneath his hands. The slick heat as he entered her body.

She was the only girl he'd ever loved. The only girl he'd ever made love to. And during those long, lonely nights, she'd become his dream girl. Sitting across from her now, watching her in the flesh brought all those fantasies back. His fingers tingled to touch her. Deep down in his groin, he ached to sink into her and revel in that closeness they'd built. Not just for the sexual release although he wouldn't mind that either. But whenever they'd been together, it had been special.

For a moment, they ate in silence. But throughout the whole cricket-chirping time, his mind shouted at him and tried to get him to change his mind about telling her good-bye.

Then she set her fork down on her plate and folded her hands together.

Because he knew her as well as he did, he predicted what she would say before the declarations were even out of her mouth. And like so many conversations they'd had in the past, he wanted to listen to every word. Not just for that sweet, sexy drawl, but because whatever she had to say was important.

Even if he might not want to hear it.

"Aiden? I can see by the look in your eyes that you have a lot going on in your mind. I know you've been through more than most people could ever even imagine. I won't tell you I understand. I won't lie and say I know how you feel."

She reached across the table and covered his hand with her own. The contrast was startling. Hers small and soft. His large and calloused.

The compassion in the simple gesture stole his breath. He'd forgotten the power of a tender touch.

A gentle moment.

A quiet calm that soothed a soul.

"What I will tell you," she continued, "is that I'm here for you. If you need to talk or even if you just need to sit and gaze out into the sky without a word. I'll be right here."

The pressure in his chest squeezed until he thought he might explode. She didn't know what she was saying. He had too much to tell—most of which was ugly and tragic.

She was a soft, sweet woman who didn't need to hear all the hideous details of what he'd been through.

When you open yourself up to talk, it will help the nightmares go away.

The advice of his PTSD counselor sprang up inside his head. Before he could stomp it down, Aiden looked across the flicker of the votive candle into the eyes of the woman he'd known since she was a sprite in pigtails.

He knew her.

Trusted her.

Believed she had a spine made of steel.

Still, he knew he had no business pulling her into his nightmare. Knew he should just say what he'd come to say and get the hell out of there. Let her go on with her life. He'd hesitated for too long now as it was.

"You sure about that?" he asked.

She gave him a slow, steady nod.

In that moment, something greater than the fight-or-flight instinct took over. While candlelight danced in her blue eyes, he took a long pull from his beer.

Maybe the time had come for him to release the claws of anguish that had dug into his soul. It wouldn't change what he'd come to tell her. Wouldn't change the outcome. But the only person he could imagine sharing his story with was Paige.

And for that, he should just call himself a selfish bastard.

Chapter Four

LIKE THE SLOW release of pressure from a teakettle, Paige listened to Aiden explain the events that had taken place in Afghanistan. As they strolled along the bank of the creek behind her house, he told her of the local people and their small villages, of the many who only desired to exist and wanted to help the American soldiers.

He told her of the Taliban, who wanted no part in making peace. He told her nightmarish tales of men, women, and children being executed in the streets for no reason. And then he told her of the day he'd watched his two best friends die.

"There's not a waking moment that I don't think about those boys." He paused, ducked his head, and shook it slowly. "Boys. Hell. They were warriors. And I was honored to be their friend."

Paige pressed her hand against her chest to hold back the wail that threatened to push through. But she would not falter. Aiden trusted her to be strong. Perhaps this was the first time he'd chosen to recount his story. She would not and could not let him down.

He stopped beneath one of the more mature trees in the orchard—her favorite place to sit and think. Dream and desire. A place where she kept one of Aunt Bertie's handmade quilts wedged into a fork in the tree and the most recent romance novel she'd chosen to read tucked inside the quilt.

Aiden reached up and inspected a ripening honey-crisp that dangled from a low branch. "And then . . . there was Rennie."

"Rennie?"

A smile pushed up the corners of his beautiful mouth, and Paige's heart stumbled.

"Renegade." He gave another slow shake of his head. "The fourth member of the three musketeers."

When he looked up, his entire expression had changed from a simple smile to a full-on grin.

"Intel was waiting for a break, and we had some rare downtime. One night after dark, the boys and I headed into the tent for a game of cards. Billy had lost three games straight. In the midst of his complaints, I heard a sound outside. When I went to check, I found this . . . puppy. This little fluff of dirty golden fur wandering around outside our tent."

"A puppy?"

He nodded. "Wasn't unusual to see dogs or cats hanging around. Looking for food. Shelter. Someone to care.

Needless to say, they don't view animals the same way over there as we do here."

His unspoken words sent a chill up her spine. She looked down at Cricket, who'd curled up at the base of the tree for a quick nap. Aiden didn't need to describe the neglect or abuse the animals there must suffer. And she couldn't bear to think of it.

"When I knelt," Aiden continued, "that dirty little pup whimpered over to me. I picked him up. When he looked at me with those deep brown eyes and licked my chin, I was a goner." He laughed, and the genuine sound gave Paige hope.

"We weren't supposed to keep a pet. For a long time, we hid him. Then, when he got too big to hide, our commander—who'd known Rennie was there all along—just turned his head. Guess he figured it wouldn't hurt anything to let me keep him. When we had to go out in the field, someone else was willing to take care of Rennie while I was gone. He offered a lot of comfort to those of us who'd been away from home for so long. But when I'd come back, Rennie would be there. He never left my side."

A slow intake of air stuttered in his chest. "Until the day they sent me home, and I had to leave him behind."

"Leave him behind?" The idea was unimaginable. "Why?"

"Not allowed to bring them to the U.S."

"That's stupid."

"Pretty much."

The shadows that veiled his eyes told Paige all she

needed to know. Leaving that dog behind had stripped him of anything left in his soul.

She curled her fingers around his arm. "Isn't there something you can do?"

The broad, strong shoulders that bore the weight of so much grief lifted in a shrug. "Someone mentioned an organization that helps bring back soldier's dogs. But there are no guarantees."

"Oh, Aiden." She pulled him into her arms and embraced him. "I'm so sorry."

"I left him with my team, and they'll treat him right." His hands settled lightly on her hips. "But all I can think about is his sitting there, wondering why I abandoned him."

Paige's heart broke in a million pieces. Aiden was not the type of man to abandon anything or anyone. Though a poor dog alone in the middle of a desert war zone wouldn't know that.

As water tumbled over the rocks in the creek and moved along the sand, Paige felt Aiden close himself off. Everything inside him seemed to be at war with the peaceful surroundings. As if he didn't deserve to be there. As if only a part of him stood on solid ground.

"Sorry." His chest expanded on a stuttered sigh. "I just really loved that dog. And I worry about him. I worry about what will happen to him when my team leaves."

"Of course you do." She pressed her cheek against his chest. Heard the unbalanced beat of his heart. She couldn't change what had happened. She could only offer him the chance to forget. "I'm so sorry."

If only for a moment.

Lifting her head, she looked up into the handsome face she'd known since before she'd learned to tie her shoes. While the moon glowed above them, a dragonfly skimmed the rippling waters, and the click-click of the cicadas surrounded them as they looked into each other's eyes.

Heat and tension pulled them together, and their lips touched on a brief kiss. He pressed his forehead against hers, and Paige curled her fingers around the back of his neck.

"I missed you," she whispered. "So much."

His dark gaze moved slowly over her face. The memories of lying in his arms, kissing him, tasting him, caught like a sigh in her chest. "Touch me, Aiden."

"My hands are dirty, Paige. I don't want—"

She knew that in his mind, he could never clean them enough to wash away what he'd had to do with them in the war. She stepped back. Instead of relief in his eyes, she saw sorrow. Hunger. Whatever battle raged within him, Paige knew she could give him the one thing he'd missed for God knew how long.

Comfort.

She grasped the bottom of her shirt and pulled it over her head. Then she reached between her breasts, unlatched the plain white cotton bra, and tossed it to the ground. She took a step forward until the tips of her breasts met with the smooth, worn cotton of his shirt.

"Touch me, Aiden." She let her fingertips waltz across his strong jawline. "Let me welcome you home like I've always dreamed."

How could he resist?

Good intentions told him to pick up her clothes and hand them back to her. Good intentions told him to walk away. She deserved better.

Good intentions did *not* move lower in his body.

Everything below his belt was running on heat, emotion, and need. He'd loved Paige the day he'd tossed his duffel on his back and headed off to basic training. He'd loved her when his boots had hit the volatile sands of Afghanistan. He'd loved her when he'd read her heartwarming letters over and over—yet he'd rarely responded.

For her sake.

He was responding now. To her inner strength. Her optimism. Her unwillingness to give up on him.

For his sake.

Paige. The woman who'd waited for him. Even when there had been a significant chance he would never come home.

For weeks, months—hell, even years—he'd dreamed of holding her close. Touching her. Tasting her. Devouring her. Holding her close and never letting her go.

Instead of walking away as he should, he curved his palms over her smooth shoulders, drew her close, and pressed his mouth to hers.

The soft touch of her lips brought him back to a place where he felt strong. Whole. And mindless of anything but his need for her. The womanly scent of her skin urged him to move forward and never look back. But that was an impossibility.

His hand slid down the curve of her spine, cupped her

bottom, and brought her tight against his erection. The instantaneous relief made him close his eyes and inhale a breath of air to clear the dizziness from his head.

She leaned into him, rose to the balls of her feet, and wrapped her arms around his neck with a sigh. His arms surrounded her, and they came together—heart to heart. His gaze swept over her plump, moist mouth, and their lips met again. Their tongues touched and danced.

And in that moment, the past simply melted away.

He could kiss her all day, all night, and it would never be enough.

Her fingers were cool as they slipped beneath his shirt to pull the fabric over his head. And then they stood flesh to flesh. Her body was warm, lush, and full of promise. Sweet memories and hope.

Desire burned inside of him as she briefly broke their embrace to grab a quilt stuck in the fork of the apple tree and spread it on the ground. And then she was back in his arms, touching him. Caressing him with heated silk that glided along his nerve endings, making his heart race, his desire spin out of control.

She unzipped his jeans, slid them down his legs, and tossed them into the increasing pile of clothes. In utter bliss, he closed his eyes as she kissed her way back up his thighs. Her long, delicate fingers embraced, stroked, and enticed his already throbbing erection. When she cupped him with gentle hands and took him into her mouth with a low hum of satisfaction, it was everything he could do not to buckle at his knees in complete surrender.

For a moment, he stood there with his hands buried

in the thick of her honey-gold hair, selfish with the need to feel whole again. But that greed only lasted a minute before he became anxious with the desire to be one with her. To bury himself deep within her warmth. To be held in her arms.

He dropped to his knees, eased her back to the quilt, and followed her down. His hands molded to her full breasts, smoothed down her luscious curves. He bent his head and kissed her mouth, then he moved lower to savor the erect tips of her breasts. She tasted like sunshine, and honey, and all the good things he remembered about being alive.

"Paige. I don't have a condom. I haven't been with anyone, but I still need to protect you."

"Shhh." She pressed a finger to his lips. "It's okay. I've got this covered. And I haven't been with anyone either."

To know she'd waited for him in every way kicked his heartbeat into a frantic race. And then, all he could do was make quick work of removing her jeans and tiny pink panties and adding them to the pile of clothes beneath the apple tree.

Her warm, soft lips danced across his chest, and she looked up at him with a smile in her eyes. "I like your tattoo."

He gave a brief glance to the eagle in flight that covered his left biceps, then leaned down and licked the small heart tattooed just above her left breast. "I like yours too."

"I put it there for you," she whispered. "Not that I'd ever forget you."

"I could never forget you either." Touched by the token

of how she felt about him, he moved over her. All thought of right or wrong disappeared, and all that mattered was being with Paige.

With their bodies pressed together, she parted her legs in invitation. When he slid inside her, he was instantly gripped by the rush of slick, moist heat. The connection they made stole his breath. It had been so damned long since he'd felt something so wonderful. And while he wanted to savor that sensation, his body did not want to concede.

He lowered his forehead to hers and kissed her until he could quell the need to pump hard for a fast release.

When his mind finally got the signal, they settled into slow, languid movements that allowed him to soak in every tiny sensation that spiraled through their connected bodies.

"I'm so glad you're home." She sighed against his ear.

For the moment, he was glad too.

Before his demons returned to mess with his thoughts, he gave Paige all his attention. He made slow, sweet love to her as if he were still the man he used to be. When they came together with a final thrust and a long moan, Aiden realized that he'd give anything to be the man Paige wanted him—needed him—to be.

But as much as he wanted it to be true, he also realized it was impossible to resurrect the dead. And the man she needed never came home.

Chapter Five

CONTENT AND SATED in Aiden's arms, Paige knew the exact moment his past came crashing down. His body suddenly tensed at the sounds of nature that had surrounded them the entire night. Yet now, he reacted as if they were the enemy.

Oh, he wasn't *showing* her any of that, but when you knew the boy before he'd become the man—the man before he'd become the soldier—it wasn't hard to see.

Her only alternative became distraction.

She rolled to her side and laid her head on his shoulder. Then she took advantage of his perfect, masculine chest and let her fingers play in the short, soft, fine hairs. "We can do that again anytime you're ready."

To her delight, he chuckled.

"I've been out of commission for so long, recovery could go either way."

"Mmmm." She leaned in and kissed him. "I'm willing to wait."

In that moment, his body tensed in a whole different way. And though she tried to drag her arm across him to hold him in place, she did not succeed. Before she could mutter the words "What are you doing?" he was up and tugging on his clothes.

Damn.

"What's the hurry?" she asked.

His hands stopped on his jeans midzip, and he looked at her through eyes filled with regret.

Dammit.

"I'm sorry, Paige."

"Don't say that." When she realized he wasn't going to come back and lie down beside her, she felt exposed and got up to dress. "There's nothing to be sorry for."

"The hell there isn't." The zipper on his jeans slid to the top, and he shook that old gray T-shirt like a flag of surrender. "I just took advantage of you."

"Are you crazy?" She yanked her T-shirt over her head. "I'm no strawberry shortcake, Aiden. I wanted you. You wanted me. That's consensual need. *Not* exploitation."

"I shouldn't have done that."

"You beautiful fool." A humorless laugh pushed past her lips. She looked up at him through the moonlight. "I've waited years for you to do exactly *that*."

"And that's the problem." He jammed his fingers into his short hair, gripped hard, then dropped his hands to his lean hips. "I didn't come see you today for *this*." He waved his hand toward the quilt on the ground.

"I know that." She folded her arms across her chest as if they would hold back all the emotions. All the things she wanted to say to him. All the words he seemed damned and determined to say to her.

"I came . . . to tell you good-bye." His tone was quiet. His words flat. Empty. Hollow. Devastating.

Her heart slammed against her ribs. "You're leaving again?"

"Not that kind of good-bye."

The finality in those words slammed into her like a speeding bullet.

"So you're not just leaving." Emotion clogged her throat, and the words came out in hoarse disbelief. "You're leaving *me*."

He glanced away as if he couldn't bear to look at her. When his gaze came back, his eyes were nearly black, like the reflection of a truly lost soul.

"I'm sorry, Paige. I'm broken. And I'm pretty damned sure nothing can fix me."

"That's bull."

He shook his head. "The person you knew, who went to war, never came back. You deserve better than what I have to give."

"The man I *knew* is standing right here. Feeding me a bunch of crap I don't believe."

"Move on, Paige. Forget about me." He glanced away again, and Paige knew even he was having a hard time believing his own words. Then those dark, haunted eyes came right back to her. "I can't love you."

"Can't? Or don't?" She sucked in a lungful of air to calm the desperation churning like acid in her heart. "Because there's a difference."

His chin dropped to his chest, and he shook his head. "Too much has happened."

"Maybe so. But you're wrong, Aiden. You're still the man you used to be. Only more." Paige kept her voice calm. Yelling wouldn't get through to him. He had to arrive at conclusions on his own. No amount of whining, crying, or persuading would do a bit of good. She just had to state the facts, then give him time. She'd already given him plenty. What were a few more days, weeks, months?

"I love you, Aiden." The confession that jumped from her mouth was not a surprise to either of them. "I always have. If I have to give you up because you've fallen in love with someone else, I'll do it. I won't like it, but I'll do it. Because your happiness means everything to me."

Her fingers curled into her palms. "But I will *not* give you up and let this sorrow swallow you and make you disappear. I can't do that."

He stood silent, looking away into the darkness. Then his eyes came back to hers, and she saw the pain. The heartache. The reluctance to actually take those steps in the opposite direction.

"*You* may have given up on you." Slowly she shook her head and held back the wash of tears that burned in her eyes. "But I *never* will."

Several heartbeats passed while they stood an arm's length away from each other in a stare-down that Paige swore she would win. At their feet, Cricket roused from her nap and gave a little whine as if she sensed the tension in the air.

Paige stood in place, resolute that she would not bend in her belief. No matter what he said or what he did.

The pressure in her chest squeezed harder as he bent at the knees and gave Cricket a brisk rub on her head. Then he stepped forward and wrapped Paige in his arms. He held her tight. Kissed her forehead. And then completely broke her heart.

"Good-bye, Paige."

Chapter Six

Good-bye, Paige?

Jesus.

Why hadn't he just chucked her on the chin or given her a pat on the back with that lame-ass exit? He'd known what had to be done. He'd been thinking about it from the moment he'd boarded the plane back to the U.S. He'd talked it over with his brother, who had called him all kinds of crazy before relenting that maybe he was right. Maybe it was time to let go of the best thing that had ever happened to him.

Right didn't make it hurt any less.

His form of a good-bye had been ludicrous and selfish. Especially when he'd said it to the woman who'd patiently waited years for him to come home.

He should never have had her get in his truck.

Should never have gone to her house.

Should never have looked at her the way he'd envisioned her in his dreams all those lonely months.

He should have kept his damn pants on and his good-bye brief.

But he hadn't done any of that.

He'd taken everything she'd offered. Made love to her like a man who planned to stay. And then he'd walked away as if she meant nothing.

Hell.

She meant everything.

Which was exactly why he'd had to walk.

He started up his truck and backed down Paige's driveway. When the tires hit the street, he looked up to the Victorian house and pictured Paige out on that big veranda, sipping sweet tea in the summer, or decorating for Christmas. Paige happy. Paige with a family. Paige with a faceless man who'd hold her close and make love to her whenever he damn well wanted.

Closing his eyes didn't take away the vision. It only made it worse.

Damn him for having such a graphic imagination.

Pressing his foot down on the accelerator spun the tires and carried him away from the only woman he'd ever loved. But that had been before life had taken a left turn and destroyed his ability to bear anything other than grief, sorrow, and guilt.

AS THE ROAR of Aiden's truck faded in the distance, Paige flopped down on the quilt that still bore his scent. The heat from his body. The sensation of being held in his arms. She looked up at the dark, cloudless sky and watched the stars twinkle as her heart shriveled into a crumpled mass. Her breathing came faster, harder, heavier, until, finally, a sob tore from her chest.

Cricket crawled onto the quilt and laid her head on Paige's stomach. Her big brown worried doggie eyes watched while Paige's tears fell.

Crying for herself was not a possibility, not when the man she loved was so completely torn up inside. Crying for *him* came easily. But her tears didn't accomplish anything other than a red nose and stinging eyes. So how could she help? How could she make a difference—a change—that would help him find his way back?

She couldn't change history. Somehow she had to find a way to help him move forward. To realize that the man he was is the same as the man he is now. Paige personally knew there were times the tasks seemed too great, too unreachable to see the brighter side.

She had learned that lesson too well when it had come time to pick the apples in her orchard. She finally figured out how to look at the orchard one tree at a time. One branch at a time. It often took her days or even weeks to put every tasty fruit into her basket, but she managed because she knew the end result–the accomplishment–would feel good.

Aiden needed to learn to feel good again. He needed to know it was okay to live, breathe, and enjoy life. She knew Bobby and Billy as well as she knew Aiden, and they wouldn't want their friend to be so unhappy. They'd enlisted together and fought side by side with the same code of honor, the same goal. But neither of those boys would have wanted Aiden to die too. They'd want him to live well and be happy. He just needed to realize that it was okay for him to do so.

So no matter what it took, branch by branch, she'd help him understand.

Pulling Cricket into her arms, Paige buried her face in her loyal friend's fur and completely opened her heart and imagination for the man she'd loved for as long as she could remember. Because living without him or not loving him wasn't an option or even imaginable.

Chapter Seven

IF YOU WANTED to get the word out in Sweet, one method worked faster than picking up the phone. Luckily for Paige, today the Digging Divas Garden Club held its monthly meeting at Bud's Diner. In two shakes of a can of whipped cream, the message would go out faster than a speedboat on smooth water.

Paige grabbed her keys up off Aunt Bertie's oak dresser and jogged down the stairs. Just like when she'd gone for her college degree or made the purchase of Honey Hill, she had a plan. Before Aiden had come back home, she'd batted a hundred. She wouldn't allow this goal to be any different. It simply meant too much.

Ten minutes later, her red F-150 slid to a gravel-spewing stop in the lot beside Bud's. She grabbed her work apron from the seat and jumped down from the truck. The lot was still half-full with late-morning coffee slurpers. In another hour, the lunch crowd would converge, and there would be standing room only. A perfect audience for when she sounded the alarm.

"I STAYED UP half the night doing Internet research," Paige said, searching the focused expressions around the crowded tables. Her heart trembled with how much they cared about the situation and how eager they seemed to want to help.

"Early this morning, I made a few calls to the organization, and they said they would look into it. Well, they work fast. Before I left for work, they called me back with the news that they can make it happen. They don't require a fee, but they do ask for donations to keep them afloat and able to help others in the same situation. I figure we need to come in around four thousand."

"Dollars?" The brim of Ethel Weber's lime green straw hat bobbled above her lavender hair.

"Hard, cold, American cash," Paige answered.

"That's nothing." Ray Calhoun lifted his old farmer's hand in a dismissive wave. "Hell, we raised ten thousand to pay for Missy Everhart's funeral when she took ill so fast."

"Can't put a dollar amount on what this will do for someone who's given so much," said Jan West, owner of Goody Gum Drops, the candy store painted like a peppermint stick in the center of town.

"But the question is . . . can we get it done before the Apple Butter Festival?" Paige asked the crowd gathered inside the diner.

"Four weeks?" Hazel Calhoun scoffed. "Easy Cheesy."

Bill McBride, Vietnam vet and local good guy stood, imposing in his leather vest and various military patches. "Consider it done." He turned to the crowd. "Right?"

The unity in the agreement that echoed across the diner sent a ribbon of warmth fluttering through Paige's heart.

Aiden might not ask for much, but the people who loved him the most were about to give him everything.

THE AXE ARCED high overhead, then slammed into the rotted tree trunk. Aiden pulled his hands back, yanked a bandana from his back pocket, and swept the cloth across his forehead.

Damn, the sun was hot today.

He'd promised his brother, Ben, that until he figured out what the hell to do with his life, he'd help out around the ranch. At the rate he was going, he didn't imagine he'd figure things out anytime soon.

It had been nearly two weeks since he'd walked out of Paige's life. Two weeks where he'd avoided anywhere he thought she might go. Two weeks since he'd slept little more than a couple of hours without dreaming of her. Two weeks where his instincts had screamed for him to get his stupid ass back in his truck and go to her. Take her in his arms. And beg her forgiveness.

Instead, he wrapped his hands around the axe handle again and dislodged the wedge from the tree stump. His instincts had been wrong before. So what the hell did he know?

Not to trust himself. That was what.

"Thought you'd be long gone by now."

Midswing, he looked up, surprised to see Paige and her dog coming toward him. Damn. The woman managed to make a pair of jean shorts and a silky little tank top look hotter than some flimsy piece of lingerie. Her hair was pulled up into a just-out-of-bed tangle on top of her head, and her smooth skin was kissed with a golden tan.

While her white tennis shoes ate up the ground, her tongue darted out to lick the half-eaten cherry Popsicle in her hand. The sudden heat whipping through his body had nothing to do with the sun above his head.

"Yeah. Me too." He watched Cricket plop her furry dog butt in the shade of a nearby tree, then he turned his gaze toward Paige. Bringing with her the scent of ripe peaches, she came to a stop in front of him. Her big blue eyes looked up at him, full of questions and a spark of her typical vibrancy.

"So why are you still here?" she asked. "Can't seem to get those boots in gear after all?"

How could he explain that while he didn't quite know where he belonged, he also couldn't bear the thought of never seeing her again? Even after telling her good-bye. Even after dodging her for weeks. How could he tell her that despite his determined words, he couldn't bring himself to just pick up and walk away?

A lump lodged in his throat as he thought of Rennie. He'd unwillingly walked away from the dog that had given him companionship and loyalty. Did he really believe he could *willingly* walk away from Paige, the woman who'd been there for him through thick and thin even if he hadn't been willing to take her up on her kindness? The woman who'd waited for him even when he hadn't been worth waiting for?

"Not sure." He shrugged and felt the sting of a sunburn on his shoulders. "I promised Ben I'd help him out. So here I am, doing hard labor while he rings up purchases of tennis shoes and skateboards down at the sporting-goods store."

Her red-stained tongue licked up the side of the Popsicle and triggered an instant reaction in his jeans.

"Is that so?" she said with a tilt of her head.

"Yep."

"Well, I'm sure Ben appreciates your help cutting this tree down. Especially since he was never one who liked to get dirty."

"Yeah." He chuckled, thinking of his brother's fastidious ways. "Never knew two kids from the same parents could be so different."

"And yet you both served in the Army."

"True."

"I always thought he'd grow up to be a lawyer or something. Some kind of professional, where he could wear a suit and tie every day."

"That's definitely more his style than cargo shorts and Hawaiian shirts."

"Have to give him credit, though. He's done a great job with the store and carrying on tradition since your father passed."

"He has done that." And why, exactly, were they discussing his brother? "So . . . what are you doing here?" he asked although he didn't mind having her in front of him with next to nothing on, smelling like heaven, and licking that Popsicle like it was . . . tasty.

The corners of her soft lips tipped as she tossed the remainder of the Popsicle to Cricket. Then she turned her blue eyes on him, swept them down his body and back up again. "I've come to make you a proposition."

A LAYER OF sweat glistened across the tops of Aiden's broad strong shoulders and highlighted that soaring-eagle tattoo. It beaded down his chest and tight, rippled stomach toward the waistband of his low-slung Levi's. Unlike the thugs one saw walking the streets of the big city, Aiden did not have a mile of underwear showing. Which only made Paige wonder if he had any on at all or if he'd gone commando. A blue bandana stuck out from his back pocket, and sawdust coated the toes of his work boots.

A low hum of need vibrated low in her pelvis. There was just something about a shirtless, sweaty, hardworking man that made her want to tear off her clothes. When that hardworking man was as gorgeous and amazing as Aiden, it was a wonder she hadn't given in to the desire. It took everything she had to compose herself and stick to what she'd come here for in the first place. Which did not include gawking at him or being tempted to stick dollar bills in his shorts.

"A proposition?" A furrow crinkled between his brown eyes.

"Not *that* kind of proposition." Although it had crossed her mind. "I'm going to respect what you said the other night even though I don't agree. Are you willing to listen to my offer?"

He leaned the axe handle against the tree trunk he'd been chopping and folded his arms across that deliciously muscular, sweaty chest. "Shoot."

She hopped up on the back of his truck and settled her behind between the steel ridges of the tailgate. "When I made the decision to buy Honey Hill, I knew I couldn't have that much property or responsibility without a good business plan. And as much as I calculated . . ." She swung her legs back and forth in time with the thoughts swinging through her brain. "I might have dreamed a little too big."

"Are you afraid of losing the place?"

"Oh. No. Nothing like that." The concern on his face forced her to quit stalling. "Part of my plan is to expand the orchard. Instead of just trying to sell apples, I want to produce apple products—butter, jelly, cider. That kind of thing. I need to do more research. Crunch some more numbers. Come up with a marketing plan. And—"

"And?" Dark brows shot up his forehead. "That's not enough?"

"Oh, you know me." She waved her hand. "Complete one project, come up with ten more."

"I do remember that about you."

The smile and slow glide of his eyes over her body said that wasn't all he remembered.

"I also intend to turn the house into a bed-and-breakfast."

"Wow. You are ambitious." He laughed, and the happy sound sent a little flutter through her heart. "But what has this got to do with me?"

"My sister has her own thing going on. And I need a partner. Someone who can help me with the follow-up, the labor, and keep the place running successfully." She hopped down from the tailgate. "You interested?"

"I'm a soldier, Paige. What do I know about cider and running a bed-and-breakfast?"

"You're smart. You love apples. You're handy with tools. And you'd make a great host because people love you."

He shook his head. "Not true."

"*Never* disregard the way people feel about you, Aiden. Sometimes . . . it's all you have."

His head came up, and something sparked in his eyes that gave her the smallest pinch of hope.

"You don't have to give me an answer right now. Just think about it." She gave a whistle to Cricket, who reluctantly got up from her cool spot beneath the tree.

Paige felt the heat of Aiden's gaze on her backside as she walked toward her truck. Someday, he'd trust his instincts. His gut. His heart. And he'd let life happen. Until then, she'd wait.

Apparently she'd become quite good at that.

"Why are you doing this, Paige?"

She turned at the sound of his deep voice, inhaled one more glimpse of that mouthwatering physique, and noted the look of complete and utter puzzlement on his face.

"We're a good team, Aiden." She lifted her hands in the air, then dropped them with a slap against her thighs. "Maybe, someday, you'll figure that out."

Chapter Eight

TWO DAYS LATER, the back screen door of Bud's Diner banged shut as Paige headed toward her truck, a hot bath, and a chilled glass of chardonnay. Sleep had evaded her since she tossed out the business proposal to Aiden, and she'd been dragging all day. Of course, most of the loss of z's had little to do with worrying whether he'd come around and say yes to picking apples and restoring her Victorian house to its former glory.

The devil might be in the details, but all Paige really wanted was for him to engage.

Every time she'd drifted off, she could see him looking back at her, his deep brown eyes filled with uncertainty and confusion. Aiden had always been a man who knew exactly who he was and what he wanted. He'd always been a man of action. Even when he'd been just a boy. It had been one of the things that had made her fall in love with him. Somewhere deep down, she knew that, no matter what, he'd always be strong. But times had changed, and the tables had turned.

It was her turn to be strong.

For him.

She untied her work apron and looked up as she approached the red F-150. Aiden stood there, lean hip braced against the back bumper, arms folded, watching her approach with a look in his eyes she couldn't quite read.

"Hey there," she said as she opened the door and tossed her purse and apron inside. "If you showed up hoping for a taste of Bud's newest concoction, you're too late. It went down the garbage disposal about an hour ago, along with a few curse words that sounded a whole lot like "Stupid effing idea."

His laugh made her smile.

"What did he come up with this time?"

"Gladys Lewis talked him into re-creating a dish she used to make for her husband back in the 1950s."

His head went back in a "Whaaaaaat?" way.

"Yeah. The fifties. An era where Jell-O molds and meat loaf were the highlight of the dinner table. Somehow, Gladys convinced Bud that tuna, potato chip, and olive casseroles were making a comeback."

"I'm speechless." He made a comical face. "And no longer hungry either."

"That's what the Calhouns said when they came in for lunch today. Much to Bud's dismay, they ignored the 'Daily Special' and promptly ordered their usual chicken fried steaks. Chester Banks said he'd brave taking a bite if Gladys could score him a date with the new cashier at the Touch and Go Market."

"Did Gladys go for that?"

"No. And neither did Chester. Or anyone else in the diner. So down the disposal it went."

"Well, at least Bud's brave enough to embrace change."

How about you? she wanted to ask, but figured he'd tell her why he was standing there looking scrumptious enough to eat in his own good time.

"Change can be good." She leaned against the side of her truck, facing him, hoping to hear some good news. "But it doesn't have to leave a bad taste in your mouth. So what brings you to Bud's parking lot?"

"You."

She liked the sound of that, and hope danced in her heart.

"I've given your business proposal some thought."

"And?" Hope was now jumping up and down, gleefully clapping its happy little hands.

His broad shoulders lifted on a slow exhale. "I'm sorry, but I'm not in any position to make promises or consider anything long-term."

"I see." Disappointment blew through her like a cold, harsh wind.

"But as long as I'm here in Sweet," he said, "I don't mind helping you out with some chores. You've done an awful lot for me, and it's the least I can do to—"

"Whoa." She raised her hands. "So . . . what? You're going to help me so you can pay back an *obligation*?"

"That's not what I said." His strong, squared chin came up. "In fact, you didn't even let me finish."

"No need. I get the point." The cold, harsh wind shifted. Hope dropped its now-sad hands. And Paige faced reality with a huge lump parked in the center of her chest. "But I don't need anyone helping me because they're taking pity on me. I don't need a handyman. I'm looking for a legitimate partner. If that's not you, then don't worry about it. I can do it myself. The last thing I'd ever want would be for you to think you owe me something for loving you."

As much as it hurt, she turned away from the frustration etched on his face, got in her truck, and drove out of the parking lot.

DUSK HAD BARELY settled over the treetops before Paige couldn't take it anymore and closed her laptop. Mr. Breene, who owned the Laundromat in town, had called on her way home and asked her to run some numbers on the tax advantages of purchasing another building on Main Street that was about to become available. Accounting was her thing. But crunching numbers became impossible when she could barely see past the flood of frustration wetting her eyes.

After pouring a glass of wine and running a bath with an extra capful of the sweet, tropical-scented bubble bath Faith had given her for her birthday, she slid into the tub until the bubbles tickled her chin. From the Bluetooth speaker sitting on the bedroom dresser, John Mayer sang "XO." How a man could make such beautiful music yet have such disastrous love affairs was anyone's guess.

Closing her eyes, she took a deep breath and waited to be swept away.

Midsong, a horrible racket crashed above the lovely strum of bad boy John's guitar. The noise came so loud and so sudden, she jumped, and water sloshed over the sides of the clawfoot tub.

"What the . . ."

The crash boomed again and even rattled the window glass. She had no choice but to get out and take a look. Either aliens had landed behind her house, or someone was demolishing her barn. Neither would be welcome.

Throwing open the window, she leaned out and took a look. In the waning light she saw a huge trailer backed up into her driveway with a cherry-picker sitting on top. Attached to the long trailer was Aiden's truck. The man himself was balanced with one long, muscular leg on the trailer bed and the other on the step of the cherry-picker while he loosened the straps securing the humongous piece of machinery.

"What the heck are you doing?"

His head swiveled around, and the thick-webbed straps in his hands stilled. For a long beat, he just looked up at her on the second floor. From her angle, she couldn't really tell exactly where he was looking or the expression on his face. His silence wasn't giving her a clue either.

"Aiden? What are you doing?" she asked again, hoping for better success this time.

She got zip.

"Stay right there, I'm coming down." She backed away from the window and closed it tight. Then and only then did she notice the big puddle of water beneath her feet. Her bare feet. Bare legs. Bare . . . crap. Now she knew what he'd been looking at.

With the exception of a few patches of bubbles, she was naked as the day she was born.

"Oh, good God, Paige." She looked into the steamy bathroom mirror. "Really?"

Disgusted with herself for the temporary loss of her mind, she grabbed her fuzzy robe off the hook on the back of the door and shoved her arms through. Her wet feet slapped and squeaked against the hardwood floor as she headed downstairs.

"You stay here," she told Cricket, as the dog and her wagging behind beat her to the door.

By the time Paige opened the kitchen door and stepped out onto the back patio, Aiden had commenced unstrapping the cherry-picker. Dodging the sharp pebbles beneath her feet, she hurried over to where he'd parked.

"Third time's a charm," she said, looking up at the magnificent view of his perfect jeans-covered ass while he bent over and unhooked the strap from beneath the machine. "What are you doing?"

He righted himself and began to neatly fold the straps. "Unhooking this cherry-picker," he drawled as though anyone in their right mind could see what he was doing.

"I can see that. The question is why there's a cherry-picker in my driveway and why is it about to be unloaded from this trailer? And why are *you* here with a cherry-picker?"

"The other day, I noticed that while most of the lower

branches of the apple trees had been picked clean, the top branches still held fruit. You've got enough space between trees to maneuver this around, and it's safer than a ladder."

"In case you've forgotten, I don't like heights. Which is why there's still fruit on the top branches. I'd rather lose the fruit than break my neck climbing a ladder." She folded her arms. "Which still doesn't explain why you're here."

"I came to help."

"I told you I didn't need your help."

He jumped down from the trailer and landed in front of her. His boots made little puffs of dirt float up into the air. "I got that message loud and clear."

"Yet you're here. With a cherry-picker."

"Yep." He flashed a smile, then turned away to unlatch another strap.

"So since you obviously heard me but didn't *listen* to me, you probably aren't going to admit you saw me hanging naked out the window either."

"Why would I deny it?" Grin fully in place, he turned back around to face her. His eyes did a quick scan up and down her body. His smile remained like he could still picture her minus the fuzzy robe. "It was the best thing I've seen all day."

"I thought someone was tearing down my barn. Or that aliens had landed."

"Those would have been really happy aliens."

When his eyebrows lifted suggestively, she chuckled. "What am I going to do with you?"

"Loaded question." He tossed the webbed strap onto

the side rail of the trailer. "For now, if you could just step back, I'll unload this thing."

"It's too dark to pick apples tonight."

"Correct. But it's here. Ready to go first thing in the morning. I don't have to have it back to the rental place until just before it closes tomorrow."

"Aiden, as much as I appreciate the thought and the effort, I don't have it in my budget to pay for this. It would just be easier to take a loss on the apples left on the trees."

"No worries. I got it for free."

"Free? How'd you manage that?"

His smile did nothing but raise more questions. "How about you back up a safe distance and let me unload this thing. We can talk later."

"Promise?"

He gave a nod toward the patio. "Now get that stuffed animal you're wearing in gear and get moving."

"Aye-aye, sir." Conceding—for now—she saluted him, then turned on her heel and, dodging those same sharp pebbles, moved up onto the patio.

For ten minutes, she sat in one of her comfy patio chairs watching Aiden in his delicious glory move in ways that showcased the power in his upper body. It was quite the show. So much so that she'd had to go inside for the glass of wine she'd started before her bath.

While Aiden worked, and she watched, her body started to hum with need. And as he brushed off his hands and headed in her direction, she wondered what it would take to convince him to forget about this whole ridiculous good-bye thing.

Maybe luck would be on her side, and all it would take would be for her to drop her fuzzy robe.

AIDEN TURNED AWAY from the parked and secured cherry-picker and moved toward Paige. One look was all it took to tell him he was in deep trouble. In her hand she held up a glass of wine for him to take. The fuzzy robe she wore had slipped off one bare shoulder, and with her legs propped up on the chair, he knew she was still naked beneath the soft fabric. The suggestive look in her eye wasn't calculated; instead, it communicated exactly the way she felt.

She wanted him.

Her unspoken message shot through his body like a burning arrow of need. Before he could let her see how much he'd been physically affected, he accepted the glass and sat down.

He wanted her too.

More than anything he'd ever wanted before. But he couldn't have her. In all fairness, he'd come to help. Not make the situation stickier.

"Sorry I interrupted your bath."

"No you're not." She smiled and sipped her wine. "Otherwise, you'd have missed me hanging out the window ready to welcome the aliens to Planet Buck Naked."

"Lucky timing for me." He shrugged. "I won't complain."

She leaned forward, and the collar of the robe slipped a little more, revealing the cleavage his fingers tingled to touch. He remembered her softness. The sweet scent of her skin. The warmth she wrapped around him. Her sighs. Her moans.

Jesus.

Everything about Paige was a sensory overload. Impossible to dismiss and hard to resist.

But resist was exactly what he needed to do.

"Now. Do you want to explain how you got the rental for nothing?" she asked. "Or maybe you could backtrack my wall of questions all the way up to what possessed you to even come up with the idea in the first place. Especially when, just a few days ago, you seemed so determined to remove yourself from my life. Now it seems you're willing to plunk yourself right back in the middle. So what's up?"

As she leaned back in her chair, Aiden knew he should come clean. He should tell her the truth. Instead, he chose to relay only a part of the truth and keep the rest to himself.

"Nothing's changed except . . . when I drove away from your house I took a good look around and saw that you could probably use a friend to help you out here and there. When you came by and tossed out the business offer, it made me understand that maybe you really are in over your head. So as your friend, I want to help out where I can."

Her eyes narrowed. "You sure toss that word around a lot."

"Which one? Help?"

"Friend."

"I hope that's what we are."

"Is that so?"

He nodded because even he wasn't sure anymore.

Friends were what they'd been in elementary school. It was what they'd been before he'd ever kissed her sweet, soft lips and discovered there were a lot better things than being just friends. Yet while he'd been in the Army and away at war, he'd been afraid of what his future held.

He'd pushed her away.

Just friends was how he'd treated her over the past several years.

No.

Scratch that.

He treated friends better than how he'd treated her. He'd rarely answered her letters. Rarely thanked her for the amazing packages she'd sent to him that he was able to share with his buddies. And though he'd told her not to, he'd *never* thanked her for putting her life on hold to wait for him. He'd dishonored the magnitude of the gift she'd selflessly given him. In return, he'd been callous, and he'd acted as if she didn't matter.

Hell. She mattered.

Sometimes, he thought she was all that mattered.

And that idea just plain scared the shit out of him because he didn't even know who he was anymore. He wasn't lying to her when he said that the man who'd left here years ago was gone. He was different. There was too much weight in his heart and on his shoulders to even remember who that guy was.

Still, cutting Paige completely out of his life seemed impossible. Especially when the first thing he woke up in the morning thinking was how much he wanted to see her smile. How badly he wanted to see that long, honey-colored ponytail swing as she walked away and gave him a great view of her curvy backside.

Sometimes in the middle of the night, he imagined the delicate touch of her fingers on his skin. The sigh she let go in the midst of laughter. Or the warmth of her body pressed against his beneath the cool sheets.

Those were his demons.

He hadn't intentionally created them, but they were there regardless.

Paige deserved someone who could give her more than just old memories. She needed fresh, new memories that would only get better and better each and every day.

So *friends* it had to be.

"That look on your face says different," she said, tilting her wineglass in his direction. "That look says there's something more than friendship at hand."

"I'm just tired." Yeah. Lame-ass excuse. Still, it was the only thing he could come up with when she looked at him the way she was, with her sleek brows pulled slightly together over those crystal blue eyes.

"Tired. Hmmm." She set her wineglass down on the table and got up from her chair. "And yet you went and rented a big ol' machine, hauled it all the way over here, and rolled it off the trailer."

Pulse throbbing, Aiden watched as she came around the table and looked down at him through eyes that held more than a hint of doubt. She touched his shoulder, just slightly, with one fingertip that then trailed up the back of his neck and down to his shoulder again. The heat of that one finger seeped through his shirt and sent an urgent message through his body.

Paige was a sexy, sensuous woman. She didn't have to work at it, she just was. And for a man who'd loved her and had tasted her passion, she was damned hard to resist.

"So . . . that's really what you want?" she asked. "To be *friends*?"

"Of course." Bullshit. With her standing so close, smelling so damned good, and looking so soft and warm, friendship was the last thing on his mind.

"But . . ." She raised one leg over both of his and straddled his lap. "*Friends*—no matter how close—don't really do this . . ." She leaned forward and pressed her lips to his forehead. Her breasts pressed against his chest, and her sweet, tropical scent wove a spell around him.

At that moment, she could do anything, and he'd be putty in her hands.

"Or this . . ." She trailed a finger down his temple to his cheek, then replaced her finger with her warm lips, which gently brushed kisses down the side of his face until they came right to his own lips.

"And they certainly don't do this." She cupped his face in her hands. At the same time, the belt on her robe loosened. The fuzzy pink fabric fell open and exposed her luscious naked body just as she kissed him. Then her tongue darted out and slowly licked the seam of his mouth.

It was the low hum of approval that vibrated in her throat that broke his resolve, and he kissed her back.

Hell yes, he kissed her back.

His hands followed suit, sliding beneath that thick fluffy fabric to touch her warm, soft skin. He pulled her close, so he could feel her hardened nipples against his chest. The movement brought her warm, damp core solid against his erection. She felt so damned good, he thought he might explode.

"You're not playing fair." He moved his palms down her backside and cupped her bare ass in his hands.

"I never said I would." She leaned in and kissed him. Their tongues danced to a tune they'd perfected over the years. Yet each time felt like the first. When he gently squeezed her bottom, she pressed down on him and moved suggestively.

Then she was gone.

In a sensuous blur, his mind registered that he was no longer holding her in his arms. Looking up through a haze of passion, he saw her sauntering away–barefoot and sexy as hell.

At the back door, she stopped to look over her shoulder with a smile. Then she dropped the robe. "Are you coming . . . *friend*?"

Point taken.

Nothing could have stopped him from following her into that house. Not even every promise he'd made to walk away and let her go.

He caught her at the bottom of the stairs and swept her up into his arms. The sound of her laughter danced in his heart. Lying near the bottom step, Cricket rolled her brown doggie eyes in a "stupid humans" expression. The dog was probably smarter than him, but he didn't let that deter him from carrying Paige up the stairs and laying her out on the bed like a delectable feast.

Completely naked, with not a shy bone in her luscious body, Paige smiled up at him. "Does this mean you've changed your mind?"

"You caught me at a weak moment."

"Then you're wearing entirely too many clothes." She snapped her fingers playfully. "Off with them, please. Let's see how close of *friends* we really can be before you change your mind again."

Change his mind?

Yeah, he probably would if his brain ever caught up with what was going on below his belt. But for now, ignorance was bliss and smelled like heaven.

He reached a hand behind him, grabbed hold of his shirt, and pulled it over his head. Not caring where it landed, he tossed it somewhere on the floor. When he reached for the button on his jeans, her hand reached out to stop him.

"Let me do that."

He lifted his hands. "Take your time."

She grinned, grabbed hold of his waistband, and tugged him closer. "Not a chance."

In his mind, the slide of a zipper never sounded so good. And the feel of her warm fingers as they curled beneath the fabric of his boxer briefs then tugged them down, never felt better.

"There's a condom in the back pocket." He might have been careless the first time, but he needed to protect her in every way possible. He'd never been with anyone else, and he knew he was as clean as they came. But accidents happened, and he refused to do anything more to mess with her future. He just needed this . . . one last time. And then he'd let her go.

"Ah." She slipped her fingers in the pocket and pulled out the foil packet. "So you did come prepared."

"I didn't intend to use it."

"Well, I do." She ripped open the packet. "And there are more in the nightstand."

He raised a brow.

"A brand-new box I purchased yesterday." She rolled the latex over his erection. "Just in case." She curled those long, warm fingers around his cock, and his eyes nearly crossed at how good it felt. For a moment, he was overcome with the sensation, and he pushed into her hand.

"God, I missed you," she whispered.

She looked so sexy sitting there, he could barely contain himself. He unwrapped the band holding her hair up on top of her head and watched as the long, honey-colored locks fell down over her bare shoulders. Her curves were full and delicious. He wanted to taste her, to devour her until she cried out his name, clawed at the bedsheets, and came against his tongue.

He reached down, curled his hand over hers, and inadvertently increased the pressure on his erection.

"Paige?"

She looked up. Apprehension filled her eyes, like she expected him to back off and walk away.

"I want you so bad I could come right now." He squeezed his hand over hers again to relieve the pressure.

"But tonight, I don't want to hurry. Tonight, we've got all the time in the world. Let's make the most of it. Okay?"

"Okay."

He leaned down, and while he kissed her, she speared her fingers into his hair. She tasted wild and forbidden as her hot, slick tongue delved deep in his mouth–stroking, caressing, and teasing. The throb of desire pulsed through his blood like a raging fire.

Tonight, they had all the time in the world, and he intended to make good use of every single second.

PAIGE HOPED THAT *all the time in the world* meant Aiden intended to stay. For a night. A day. A week. Forever. But right now, she'd take what she could get. There had never been a doubt in her mind that they belonged to each other. Not even when he'd ignored her letters or the fact that she'd waited so long for him to return.

Hopefully, he'd stop playing games with himself and realize that too.

"You're so beautiful," he said, lifting her hair over her shoulders and sliding his fingers through the long strands. "Even after all those months in the sand, I could still picture you when I closed my eyes. And you smell so damned good. I could bury my face in your skin and stay there forever."

Staying in his arms forever sounded like a darned good idea.

When he trailed kisses down her neck to the sensitive spot near her shoulder and sucked her skin into his mouth, she knew *all the time in the world* was going to be tough to pull off. All she wanted was him, inside her, pushing, and pounding their way to completion.

"As long as you bury yourself inside my body too . . ." She slid her hands down his strong torso and cupped his firm buttocks in her palms. "You have a deal."

"Oh, that will definitely happen. But right now, I want to taste you." He covered her breasts with his hands. Her nipples peaked beneath the warmth of his skin, and she moaned deep in her chest as he gently pushed her back onto the mattress. "All over."

"Works for me."

A chuckle parted his lips, then he paid very careful attention to each erect nipple with gentle pulls of his hot, moist mouth. Slowly, seductively, he kissed his way down her body. And when he hit home between her legs, he took his time. He licked. Stroked. Sucked. And had her mindlessly begging for that slow burn that was just out of reach.

Thrusting her hips was a natural reaction to the increasing friction of his tongue. When he slipped his hands beneath her butt and pulled her closer to his mouth, she exploded with a cry. The fireworks of shocks and tingles that burst from her core and danced through her blood stole her breath. Left her speechless.

Still, she wanted more.

She reached for him. Pulled him up. Then she reached between them, wrapped her fingers around his long, thick erection, and squeezed. "I want this." She panted. "You. So bad. Right now."

"Not as bad as I want you." He wrapped his arm around her waist and turned her over onto her knees. "I remember you like it this way."

"Yes." She looked over her shoulder at this strong, virile, sexy man as he kissed his way across her shoulders and down her back. Just the sight of him set the tingling in her core to ready, set, go mode. "I like it when you take me like this. Make me yours, Aiden."

A low growl rumbled from deep in his chest. He clasped his hands around her hips and pulled her against him as he entered her from behind. His rigid, thickness completely filled her and felt so damned good, she cried out.

He retreated, stopping just short from pulling out, then he repeated the process—building a pressure so sweet, so hot she didn't know how long she'd last.

Arching her back to make the angle even more interesting, she looked over her shoulder. The responding look on his face was a combination of determination and ecstasy. He looked hot, muscular, and sexy. And that turned her on even more.

And then, as he'd always done, he put her first.

While his hips pumped faster and their skin slapped together, he reached around and found her most sensitive hot spot with his fingers. In perfect unison, he stroked, swirled, and pumped hard. When she came, it was with such a force that a guttural sound ripped from her chest. A moment later, he gripped her hips, pumped harder and faster, then echoed her groan of utter satisfaction.

When they finally fell together in a heap of wobbly

muscles and tingling sex, she laughed. "Remind me to find you in a weak moment a whole lot more often."

He pulled her back up against his chest and kissed her shoulder. "Sweetheart, where you're concerned, I'm always weak. And I'm not complaining."

SOME NIGHTS WERE torture. Paige had lost count how many she'd spent looking up at the ceiling and wishing the noisy cicadas would drown out the worry that kept her awake. For countless nights, she'd wondered if Aiden would ever come home. And if he did, would he ever come home to *her*.

Last night had been the slice of heaven she'd prayed for all these years.

Making love with the man was one of those miraculous moments that left her greedy for more. Sleeping in his embrace went beyond words but also left her wanting more. It didn't take a genius to realize she just wanted more of him, period.

Realizing his side of the bed was cold, she rolled over and found it empty. A shiver crawled through her heart.

When had he left?

And, more importantly, why?

Just then, the quiet of the early morning was shattered by the hum of an electric motor. Paige padded over to the window and looked out to find Aiden inside the cherry-picker, hovering near the treetops with several overflowing baskets of apples by his boots.

In a repeat of last night, she opened the window and

leaned out, buck-naked for any possible invading aliens and especially Aiden to see.

"How about a cup of coffee?" she called out to be heard about the motorized hum.

His head whipped around, and as soon as he saw her, a huge grin spread across his face. "Stay right there. I've got a better idea."

By the time she closed the window and turned around, the thumps of his boots were coming up the stairs. When he entered the bedroom, he executed a softer version of one of the tackles he used to exhibit playing football in high school, and they ended up on the bed again.

And then he kissed her.

When they came up for air, he pulled off his clothes and climbed beneath the sheets with her. Tucked her beneath his warm body and kissed her neck.

She laughed. "You smell like apples."

"You smell like I'm about to get lucky."

"As long as you know your place in the universe."

"I don't know about the universe. But I promise, with you, I definitely know where I fit."

With one smooth stroke, he made good on his promise. So good in fact, she had no choice but to sigh out loud.

Chapter Nine

It HAD TAKEN days for Aiden to pick the rest of Paige's apples. Sure, it might not have taken quite as long if she hadn't kept distracting him by leaning naked out the window. Or bringing him glasses of sweet tea in that nothing little tank top and cutoff jeans. Or tempting him with warm, fresh-baked cookies—in bed.

In fact, it hadn't taken half as long as picking the apples did to realize he'd spent nearly every waking hour either by her side, on top of her, or inside her.

In the mornings, they shared long conversations over coffee. At night, they moved those meaningful chats out to the back patio. And between the times they made love, they'd talk some more. Aiden wondered now how he'd survived all those months without Paige to talk to. Somehow, she managed to get him to open up. To share. And it felt good. Just like his PTSD counselor said it would.

In Afghanistan, he'd transferred his devotion to

Rennie. Although the dog would often just cock his head at some of the things Aiden would say, he'd been a good friend and a great listener.

Aiden missed the hell out of him.

Having Rennie back in his life would make everything complete. But that would never happen. The military wouldn't bring his dog back. No matter how much Aiden had begged, bargained, and pleaded, the answer had been a resounding *no*.

The knowledge that he'd never see his friend again just made his damn heart start to ache all over. And it was that missing piece of the puzzle that made him realize that no matter how hard he tried, he'd never feel whole. Never feel complete. Not even when he was lucky enough to have the love of a good woman.

While Aiden strolled through the Touch and Go Market with a cartful of groceries to replace the ones he'd devoured at Paige's house, he realized that being with her was a hell of a way to feel good. To forget. It was the only time he actually allowed himself that privilege. But not a moment went by when he didn't battle the demons that reminded him that he needed to let her go. Trouble was, he didn't know if he was strong enough to make it happen.

"There you are!"

Aiden turned away from studying the ice-cream section of the freezer for just the right flavor to smear all over Paige's body so he could lick it off. With orthopedic shoes squeaking and in all their flowered muumuu glory, Gladys Lewis and Arlene Potter, president and copresident of the Sweet Apple Butter Festival committee, came toward him at full speed.

"Ladies."

"Aren't you just a sight for my eyes," Arlene said, running a wrinkled hand across his biceps.

"That's not the right saying, Arlene." Gladys frowned at her lifelong friend in a way that made the red smear of her lipstick look slightly scary.

"I don't care what the saying is supposed to be." Arlene scoffed. "I'm too busy looking at the pretty package."

Aiden had never felt like a piece of meat before, but Arlene's disconcerting once-over definitely pushed him in that direction.

Maybe he was just imagining things.

After all, Gladys and Arlene were beyond their golden years and heading into ancient status. They weren't your typical sweet old ladies. Most folks in town said the BFFs leaned more toward the "looking for trouble" type. Still, he supposed he could just be blowing things out of proportion. Most likely they were just . . . spirited.

Even as Arlene continued to feel up his biceps, *spirited* was the expression he chose to use for them. Because God help him if there was anything more.

"We came here for a purpose," Gladys insisted. "Quit yer pussyfootin' around."

"Oh, all right. Ya big old party pooper." Arlene gave his arm a final squeeze with a wink. Then she did some kind of weird shoulder wiggle. "You ever need some . . . company, handsome. You come find me."

Aiden had never been more curious. Appalled. Or afraid.

"We need your help, young man." Gladys wrapped her arthritic hands around his cart and started to push it down the aisle. Arlene followed with her orthopedic shoes squeaking loudly above the Muzak version of the old nineties hit "I Wanna Sex You Up."

No doubt life could be odd. And Aiden had to wonder if somehow he'd fallen into the Twilight Zone.

"Where are you going with my groceries?" he asked after he followed them around the aisle cap stocked with graham crackers, marshmallow cream, and supersized bars of chocolate.

"We got to talk business," Gladys said, grabbing a jar of marshmallow cream and tossing it in his basket. What the hell was he going to do with marshmallow cream? "Can't do it in the middle of the frozen-food aisle."

"Pshaw." Arlene looked up at her cohort and tossed a bottle of caramel sauce in for good measure. "I've done *it* in the middle of the frozen-food aisle before."

Oh, dear God.

Fearing for his life, or at least his sanity, he followed them. Because the hell if his curiosity would allow him to stay put.

"MARSHMALLOW CREAM?" PAIGE cocked her head as he pulled the groceries from the bag.

"Wait. It gets better."

As he set the container of ice cream on the counter, then the caramel sauce, Paige asked, "Are we having ice-cream sundaes?"

A jar of maraschino cherries followed up her question, and he looked up to catch the humor in her eyes.

"*You* are the ice-cream sundae," he said. "And as much as I'd like to take credit for it, you can thank Gladys and Arlene for the idea."

"I . . . don't know what to say."

"On second thought, scratch that." He folded his arms across his chest. "They didn't give me the idea, they just dumped everything except the ice cream in my cart and told me what to do with it."

Paige giggled.

"I can only take credit for the ice cream."

"I guess I should be aghast that those two told you what to do with all this."

"I know. They kind of freaked me out a little."

"Those two never fail to surprise me." She came toward him and danced her fingertips up his chest. "However, I'm appalled they didn't think you could come up with the idea all on your own."

Her sweet, smiling mouth was so close he just had to kiss her.

"Maybe they think I have too much sand in my brain from being in Afghanistan too long."

"Maybe they just don't know you as well as I do." She rose to her toes and took their brief kiss to another level. "Then again, maybe I just need a little reminder."

Curling her fingers into the front of his shirt she started pulling him toward the stairs.

"Wait a minute!" He broke free long enough to grab the ingredients for a good time off the counter, then raced her to the bedroom.

ALL WAS RIGHT in the world when you had a half-empty container of ice cream melting on the nightstand and a completely empty bottle of caramel sauce on the floor.

In broad daylight.

Paige gave a happy sigh.

"We really can't keep doing this, you know," Aiden said. "It's not good for you."

"Not good for me?" The vibrations still humming through her body after that knock-your-eyes-to-the-back-of-her-head orgasm felt pretty damned good. "I don't believe I ever mentioned being on a diet."

His silence indicated that party time was over, and his tenacious demons had just entered the room.

"Oh. Wait. Are we back to your leaving again? Have we opened the door and let all your doubts in on our private moment?"

"I don't mean to."

She raised up on one elbow. "But you just can't help yourself. Is that it?"

"I just get to thinking—"

"Then stop thinking."

"I can't, Paige." He closed his eyes and laid his arm across his forehead.

"Aiden. You just licked ice cream and caramel sauce off my body. We just had amazing sex. Don't you feel good about that?"

"Yes." His jaw clenched.

"And that's the problem, isn't it?"

God, he just broke her heart.

"You're too afraid to let yourself feel good." She knew he wasn't alone in the way he felt. There were thousands of soldiers who had returned from war broken in some way, whether physically, mentally, or emotionally. She knew it, but it didn't make it any easier to accept that the man she loved was hurting so deeply, and there was little she could do about it.

"You're an amazing woman, Paige." He rolled to his side, cupped her face in his hand, and stroked his thumb across her cheek. "Your patience is beyond comprehension. Being with you is the only place I feel at home. Your smile and your laughter take away all the pain. Temporarily. And that's the problem. It's not a slight on you. You're not the problem. I am."

So often in a troubled relationship, those words rang empty. But with Aiden, she knew they were true. Everyone had baggage. Aiden's had just been over-packed.

"When I close my eyes . . . when I'm not looking right at you," he said. "When I'm not touching you . . . it all comes crashing back. The sight of my friends being blown into the air. The sound of their screams. The smell of their blood. I miss my friends, Paige. I miss my dog. I miss feeling . . . normal. And I'm so damned afraid I'm never going to feel that way again. I don't want to drag you into my own personal hell. It's not fair to you."

Paige let go of the breath that clogged her chest. She kissed his forehead, then his lips. "You'll find your way back. I know you will. And I'll be right here whenever you need me."

"I don't want to just use you," he said. "That's the problem. It can't be all about me. If we're together, it's an us. But . . . I just don't know if I can carry that weight right now."

She chuckled to break the tension in the air. "Are you calling me fat?"

"No. I'm calling you wonderful. Amazing. Perfect. But I need to be someone you can count on. Someone you know will be there for *you* when you need someone."

"I understand."

He kissed her again, then got up off the bed. "I should probably grab a shower and get out of here. I know you've got things to do."

"There's nothing more important than you."

"You're wrong, baby." He leaned down and kissed her again. "There's nothing more important than *you*."

When he turned toward the bathroom, she somehow managed to keep her tears at bay. "Aiden?"

He stopped and looked over his shoulder.

"I'll be right here. Always."

Chapter Ten

A WEEK LATER, Aiden stepped from the shower, wrapped a towel around his waist, and went in search of something decent to wear that wasn't camo or threadbare cotton.

After he'd been cornered at the Touch and Go Market by Gladys and Arlene and shocked to his toes over the whole ice-cream-sundae bit, they'd asked him to be a judge in the festival's apple-butter competition. Apparently, the prior year there had been a controversy due to favoritism.

How could he refuse the passion behind their request? At least it momentarily diverted Arlene's passion for his biceps.

But now, when he'd rather be enjoying the festivities from where he could blend into the background, he'd be thrust in the spotlight. With respect, he would listen to all the nice things people had to say about his serving in the military, while deep inside he thought of himself as a total screwup. He'd failed his best friends. He'd abandoned his dog. And he'd disappointed Paige.

Jesus. He was batting a thousand.

With a long groan, he turned his attention back to matters he could control. There were two sets of clothing choices in his closet. Military and ultracasual. Not much in between. He grabbed a freshly laundered button-down shirt off a hanger, then went to raid his brother's closet for a pair of khakis.

Ben came around the corner in the hall and stopped in his tracks. "I don't mind sharing a house with you as long as you don't run around in your underwear."

Aiden laughed. "I was just on my way to steal a pair of pants from you."

"Got a hot date?" Eyes dark like his own assessed his face, looking for a clue behind Aiden's getting dressed up in the middle of the day.

"Judging the apple-butter contest at the festival."

Ben crossed his arms. "How do *you* rate?"

"Arlene Potter likes my biceps."

"Arlene Potter likes everyone's biceps."

"Yeah. She and Gladys kind of take crazy old lady to another level."

"Ah, they're harmless." Ben walked into his room, grabbed a pair of khakis from his closet, and tossed them to Aiden.

"Easy for you to say," Aiden said. "Arlene wasn't feeling you up in the ice-cream aisle."

"Thank God. You taking Paige to the festival?"

"No."

"Meeting her there?"

"Nope."

"Why the hell not?"

"None of your business."

"You're living in my house. That gives me the right to be nosy. So why the hell aren't you taking Paige to the festival?"

"Because . . ." Aiden poked his legs through the pants and looked down to zip them up. "I'm trying to let her go."

A whack upside the head knocked him off balance.

"What the hell did you do that for?" Aiden put a hand to the area of attack.

"Knocking some damned sense into that thick frickin' skull of yours."

"I've got sense."

"Bullshit."

"I do. Which is exactly why I'm trying to back away. She deserves a great life, Ben. I can barely figure out what I'm going to do on a day-to-day basis."

"Exactly."

"What? That doesn't even make any sense," Aiden said. "If that's what you believe, then you should be on my side and see the situation like I do."

"No, little brother. What I *believe* is that you and Paige belong together. You always have. And what I *see* is the smile on your face when you're around her. If a woman can do that to your heart, who the hell do you think is going to help you mend? If you're looking to find your place in this world–where you belong–look no further than her."

Aiden hesitated because he always hated to admit his brother was right. But in this case, he was definitely right. "I guess that makes sense."

"*Guess?*"

Ben went to take another swipe at him, but Aiden was quicker and backed away.

"I *guess* you should get your sorry ass in gear and go find her," Ben said. "Make her yours before she wises up and dumps you."

"I still think she'd be smart to do just that."

Ben frowned.

"But hopefully, I'm not stupid enough to actually let that happen."

Ben yanked him into a hug. "The war fucked with all of us, little bro. I just want you to be one of those who came home and found his way back into a happy life. I love you, man.

"Love you too."

The mutual backslapping emotionally got to both of them, and they backed away from each other. A split second later, Aiden grabbed up his keys, headed toward his truck, and hoped he would not be accused of favoritism if Paige had entered the apple-butter competition this year.

Because in his books, hands down, she was a winner.

And he was damned lucky she loved him.

A WIDE VARIETY of SUVs, trucks, and economy cars were parked bumper to bumper along the curb at the Town

Square–better known as the entertainment hub of Sweet. Whether it was a birthday party, battle of the bands, or the Fourth of July picnic, it happened in the little park smack-dab in the center of town.

Though the latticework gazebo had seen better days, and the trees were tall and ancient, the folks mingling around the grass lot filled the square with spirit and a sense of renewal.

Aiden glanced past the rainbow of canopies, where vendors hawked everything from scented candles to homemade cinnamon rolls and handmade animal puppets. Over the brims of sun-deflecting Stetsons and ball caps, he scanned the area to find the banner that would lead him toward the apple-butter-judging area.

In the distance, someone on the loudspeaker called out a winner of the cakewalk. He finally spotted the big yellow "Judging Zone" sign. The huge crowd gathered in front of the area made him worry that he might be late. A quick glance at his watch verified he was right on time.

As he started toward the crowd, the two elderly charmers who'd conned him into the gig appeared like magician's assistants.

"My, my. Don't you look handsome." Gladys Lewis grinned up at him through wrinkly lips smeared with bright red.

"Shucky-darn. We thought you might have worn your uniform." Arlene Potter gave him a leering once-over before grabbing onto his arm and giving it a squeeze. "But as long as these sleeves are short, and we can see these yummy muscles, we don't mind."

Hoo-boy.

"I apologize, ladies. I'm no longer a member of the military. So I'm not allowed to wear the uniform."

"Good Lord." Gladys gave her cohort a whack with her lace fan. "You knew that, Arlene."

"I'm sorry."

Not wanting to cause the elderly women to feel uncomfortable, Aiden flashed them both a smile.

"Too bad, though," Arlene added with a wink. "Nothing hotter than a man in uniform."

"Good heavens." Gladys rolled her faded blue eyes. "Come on, young man. Pay no attention to her. She's just getting old, and her marbles don't always roll in the same direction."

The women in their floral muumuus and straw hats hooked their arms through his and led him toward the crowd. As they drew closer to the gazebo, the festival attendees turned toward them and began to part like a gaping zipper.

The whole scene felt odd, and a tickle of alarm crept up the back of his neck. Had it not been for the friendly faces turned his way, he might very well have made a beeline in another direction.

"It's okay, Lieutenant Hottie. We're just glad to have you home." Arlene gave him a light pat on his arm. He looked down into the reassuring smile on her weathered face. She gave a nod toward the gazebo. "Some of us more than others."

When Aiden looked up, he saw Paige in a floaty yellow sundress. Her hair had been pulled back in a long braid, tousled by the summer breeze. Her beautiful mouth lifted at the corners. Aiden swore he'd never seen anything prettier in his life. As she held her hand out for him to join her, his heart went warm and fuzzy.

Gladys and Arlene blended back into the crowd, and he took a few steps forward. It was then he realized Paige wasn't reaching out to him. She was letting go of a yellow ribbon that slowly fluttered toward the ground. His gaze followed the ribbon down to the green grass and the large golden dog that sat back on his haunches like the most patient soldier.

Aiden's heart leaped into his throat, and the ever-present ache in his chest vanished. In a rush of disbelief, he dropped to his knees.

"Rennie!"

The retriever's massive paws dug into the earth, and, within a warm flash of sunshine, Aiden had his arms around his friend's soft, silky neck. Rennie whined, and wiggled, and did a happy-doggie dance.

If dogs could smile, Rennie had a full-on grin. Aiden did too as Rennie's long tongue slurped up the side of his face.

"I've missed you, boy."

Aiden thought of all the nights he'd shared his cot with a scared little pup. One who'd grown so big, Aiden had considered sleeping on the ground when that cot became too small for the both of them. They'd seen hell together. Shared sorrow. They'd even shared meals. He gave the dog a kiss on the top of his head and laughed at the exultant bark he received in response.

With another lick to Aiden's face, Rennie flopped down on his side and rolled over for a shameless belly rub.

Forgiven.

Just like that, Rennie forgave him for leaving him behind.

Aiden curled his fingers in the dog's thick fur and did his best to hide the tears swimming in his eyes. When he looked up, Paige came toward him, with Cricket prancing on a leash by her side.

Paige looked at him with her big blue eyes and smiled. "Welcome home, Lieutenant Marshall."

"Welcome home," the rest of his community cheered.

If there had been any lingering doubt of where Aiden belonged, who he belonged to, or whom he belonged with, it dissipated right then and there.

He stood. "How did you find him?"

"*We* found him," she said. "Eagerly waiting to be brought home to you."

"*We?*"

"Sweet." She gave a nod to those surrounding them. "All the people you went off to protect. All the people who've been waiting to welcome you home. They all came together and made this happen . . . because I told them how much you love this dog. And because they love you." She tilted her head back and smiled. "Of course, not nearly as much as I do."

A smile burst from his heart as he looked at the faces surrounding him. "I don't know how to thank you. Or how to repay you."

"You owe us nothing in return, Lieutenant Marshall."

Bill McBride stepped forward. "You've paid your dues. Just be happy."

Aiden curled his fingers in Rennie's thick fur, wrapped his arm around Paige, and gave the Vietnam vet who'd seen plenty during his own tour of duty, a nod. "I'll do what I can."

Paige flashed him a smile, then turned it toward the crowd. "All right. Y'all have seen enough. Judging starts in thirty minutes."

As the crowd slowly dispersed, Aiden shook his head. "Do they always mind you like that?"

"If they want fresh pickles and crunchy lettuce on their burgers, they do."

He smiled, gazed down into the passion and comfort in her eyes, and brushed a long tendril of honey-gold hair away from her face. His friends—better men than him—had not made it back home. But he would not dishonor their memories–the freedom they'd fought for–by taking life and all it offered for granted.

He was grateful to have an opportunity to love Paige for the rest of his life. And there was no time like the present to make that happen.

If she'd still have him.

"I'm in," he said.

Her softly arched brows came together. "*In?*"

"The partnership. I'm taking you up on your offer if it's still on the table."

"Of course it is."

"Good." He tugged her closer. "Then I accept. On two conditions."

"Which are?"

"I pay my half up-front. Equal partners."

"That's one condition." Her hand slid up to his shoulder. "What's the other?"

"We make it permanent."

She leaned her head back as though he'd offended her. "I would never offer you half the business if I didn't expect it to be long-term."

"Not the business. You and me." He lowered his mouth to hers, not caring if they had an audience or if the whole world watched. He kissed her with everything he felt in his heart. When he raised his head, he said, "We're a good team."

"Yes. We are." Her warm fingers caressed the side of his face. "I'm glad you finally figured that out."

"I needed to have several talks with myself to make that happen. And a whack upside the head from Ben didn't hurt either."

"You know, you're quite the negotiator." Her smile warmed him all the way down into his heart. "If you're looking for something to do, maybe you should think about running for mayor in the fall."

"Mayor?"

"Why not?" The music of her laughter danced across his skin. "You've proven to be quite a service-oriented kind of guy. Running the town should be easy after what you've been through."

"I might be too busy to be mayor." He nuzzled her sweet-scented neck.

"You keep that up, and I guarantee you *will* be too busy."

A playful bark interrupted them, and they both looked down to where Rennie was snuffling Cricket's ear.

"Looks like Rennie's already quite at home here." Paige laughed. "He might have even found love."

"He's not the only one." Aiden caught her hand in his and kissed her fingers. "*You're* home to me, Paige. And while I may never be the man I was before I left here—"

She pressed a finger to his lips. "That's okay. I'm not the same woman."

No she wasn't. She was more. More than he ever expected. More than he deserved. She was a gift he'd treasure always.

"I love you, Paige. I always have. And I want to be with you for the rest of my life. If you'll have me." He gave her hand a squeeze. "Say yes."

"Oh, Aiden. It's always been yes." She lifted to her toes, wrapped her arms around his neck, and kissed him. "Always."

Can't get enough of Candis Terry's
sexy, delightful Sweet, Texas?

Next summer, return to watch as the last
Wilder to wed finally meets his match in

TRULY SWEET

War had been hell for Marine Sergeant Jake
Wilder. He'd lost his big brother, his best friend,
and now he was fighting his way back from an
injury that had nearly cost him his own life.
He'd once considered himself a military lifer,
now he needs to rethink his entire future.
But that definitely doesn't include a certain
opinionated blonde who's been a pain in his
backside for as long as he can remember.

Annie Morgan thought she'd found her Prince
Charming, only to discover he'd been a toad
all along. Abandoned and a new mother,
she doesn't have time to think about finding
her happily ever after. And there's no way it
would come in the form of a gorgeous Marine
with a chip on his shoulder a mile wide. But
sometimes fate has a mind all its own.

SUMMER 2015

Chapter One

Two months, three surgeries, and a stint in a military rehab hospital later, Jake kicked up gravel and dust in his black Chevy truck with the radio blasting Montgomery Gentry's "Hell Yeah." He flew down the proverbial long and winding road past the ranches that dotted the landscape with wide-open meadows and grazing longhorn cattle. Past the landmarks of Sweet, Texas, and the memories of his youth, where he and his brothers had raised more than a little hell while having the time of their lives.

In no hurry to be anywhere in particular, he turned the truck onto Main Street and cruised past the old water tower, where any high-school kid worth their weight in rebellion went to drink beer. At the stop sign while he waited for a young mother and her three small children to scurry across the street, he looked over to Sweet Surprise, the thriving cupcake and ice-cream shop his former sister-in-law Fiona owned. He thought about stopping in to sample his favorite flavor, but this morning his stomach rumbled for more than a sugary treat. Today, his taste buds hankered for the gut-bomb meal he'd craved all those months he'd eaten sand sandwiches in Afghanistan. Not to mention the bland fare called hospital food while they'd had his leg hijacked in some kind of futuristic contraption.

Maybe a burger dripping with cheese wasn't going to change the world or make him forget that the Marines had kicked him to the curb with what they'd politely termed an honorable discharge, but it would satisfy his hunger and momentarily get him away from the lovable hovercraft he called Mom.

His reentry into civilian life had taken place two days ago. During those forty-eight hours, he'd been overwhelmed by the surge of love and attention from family and friends. Not that he didn't appreciate it. But from the moment he'd walked through the front door of Wilder Ranch, the calls and visitors had been nonstop. The casseroles and desserts had piled up on the kitchen table until it looked like either someone had died, or they were preparing for one of the famous Wilder Family BBQ Blowouts.

All the while, his mother had barely taken her eyes off him. Though his healing and progress had been good, he still walked with a cane, which apparently communicated a distress signal to the woman who'd given him life. Mama Bear kept such a close eye on him, he figured any minute she'd put bumper guards on all the hard-surfaced furniture like she had when he'd been a kid.

Just this morning, he'd needed a moment of solitude

and had gone into the barn to brush down Rocky, his favorite quarter horse. In two blinks, his mother rushed out to *check on him*. Jake had felt his throat tighten and a streak of panic grip his chest. While he appreciated the love and thoughtfulness, he was having a hard time adjusting to all the fuss.

He wasn't broken, he just needed a break.

A moment to forget the bad and remember the good. To find his way back into the rhythm of life—one that had nothing to do with military routines, high-powered weapons, and the enemies of mankind. To find the joy and laughter that had once been the foundation of his life.

Minutes later, he rolled the truck to a stop in the gravel lot beside Bud's Nothing Finer Diner. The exterior was little more than a yellow concrete box with a neon sign. But the interior overflowed with character and a patriotic red, white, and blue décor that shouted "Don't Mess With Texas" from every corner. No question he'd be walking into a bird's nest of gossip. Bud's was *the* place the townsfolk gathered to mourn, celebrate, discuss local politics or who was sleeping with whom.

From his open window, the aroma of grilled burgers and fresh apple pie made his mouth water. When he opened the truck door, he realized that getting down from the damn thing might not be as easy as getting up. He hadn't thought of that earlier when he'd climbed inside. His thigh muscles were healing in a way that made moving in one direction easy. The opposite direction, however, was like letting Freddy Krueger use him as a scratching post.

Thankful no one was in the parking lot to see him struggle, he maneuvered down to the ground, curled his fingers over the head of the cane, and controlled his uneven gait as he headed inside.

Bud's might be Sweet's breeding ground for chitchat, but he hadn't come looking for gossip, sympathy, or acknowledgment.

He'd just come for a burger and a milk shake.

Before he could reach for the door handle, the door swung outward. Holding it open from the other side was Chester Banks, Sweet's very own playboy octogenarian. The man had more nose than face these days, and his smile often displayed a set of false teeth that didn't always stay put, but he gave Jake a respectful nod as Jake maneuvered into the diner with as little detection as possible.

"No need to thank me," Chester said. "Been in about the same place as you. Got my scrawny ass shot up stormin' that damn beach in World War II. Sure puts a hitch in yer giddyup, but it coulda been worse, I guess."

"True that." Jake had no idea the old guy had ever served in the military, let alone one of the toughest wars ever battled. Of course, as a soldier himself, he knew there were two kinds of veterans; those who loved to tell war stories, and those who wanted to bury the memories deep. As easy as it was to poke fun at Chester's flirtatious ways, at least the old codger was still around to make it happen.

"Thanks just the same," he said, as Chester gave him another nod and left the diner.

While Jake made his way to a booth, he got a two-finger salute from Bill McBride, a Vietnam vet, and a chin lift from Ray Calhoun, both of whom were sitting at a table, playing a game of checkers. At the big round table in the back, the Digging Divas Garden Club looked up in surprise. Instead of their usual exuberance, most just smiled as though they realized he might need some space. The tear sliding down Arlene Potter's crinkly cheek could have been from allergies. Or it could have been because, even at her advanced age, Arlene loved a man in uniform. Not that he was wearing one. But that really didn't matter to Arlene. She had a vivid imagination.

Jake tried to relax. He hadn't known exactly what he'd be walking into here, but the silent acknowledgments worked just fine for him.

With his favorite booth vacant, he eased over to the middle of the red vinyl seat and stretched his leg. As he looked out the window at the passersby on their way through their daily routines, he took a breath to ease the ache slicing down his thigh. Moments later, a menu sailed onto the table in front of him, and a cup of ice water landed without a splash.

His head instantly came up.

Blue eyes focused, Annie Morgan stood there, weight balanced on one hip while she tapped the eraser of her pencil against the order pad.

In the past couple of years, the Wilder family had expanded with three of his brothers having said the I do's. Thanks to his brother, Jackson, and her sister, Abby, he and Annie were now related by marriage. Before that, they'd been adversaries for as long as Jake could remember. Always outspoken and not a stranger to butting in where she didn't belong, they'd gone head-to-head on many outlandish subjects. If he said the sky was blue, she'd argue it was turquoise. If he said a steak would take seven minutes to grill, she'd say five. If he said the Rangers would win by a home run, she'd bet they'd lose with a strikeout. It seemed like the girl just liked to argue. More often than not, he'd rise to the bait. Just as he always did with his brothers. One of these days, he'd learn to just sit back and smile.

Today probably wasn't that day.

"Forget something?" Her eyes narrowed just slightly, and the silky blond ponytail hanging down her back swung to the side as she tilted her head in a way that suggested she was primed for a challenge.

"Not that I'm aware."

"Uh-huh." She tucked the stub of a standard yellow pencil behind her ear. "Guess you've been away too long to remember that most folks walk in here wearing a smile. Looks like you left yours at home."

"Guess I'm just not much in the mood."

"Seriously?" Her eyes narrowed a bit more, yet somehow a shower of silver sparks still managed to flash. "Why?"

He hated to use the word *Duh*, but it seemed so apropos.

"So . . ." Her shoulders lifted and dropped. "What? You're going to let that walking cane snuff out the eternally grinning smart-ass that lives inside you?"

Her comment hit its mark with stinging success.

Jake clenched his teeth and lowered his gaze to the laminated menu he'd been able to recite by heart since he'd been twelve. "Annabelle, how about you go away and give me a minute to look over the menu?"

"Because that would be a total waste of time, *Jacob*."

His gaze jerked up again just as she shifted her weight to a position she probably intended as a show of obstinacy. Yet all it really managed to do was push her full breasts against that snug white *Bud's Diner* T-shirt. Instinctively, his gaze dropped lower to the little black skirt hugging nicely rounded hips and the pair of tanned, shapely legs that ended with the sparkly blue sneakers on her feet. Liking what he saw, his gaze took that same slow ride back up her body.

When the hell had little Annie Morgan grown up and gotten so curvy?

"You can stare at that menu all day long," she said through lips that were pink, plump, and glossy. Lips that looked like they needed to be kissed.

The unexpected and unwanted thought was like a splash of ice water in his face. Annie had been a pain in his backside for as long as he could remember. The last thing he should be doing was thinking about her damned mouth. Or her curvy body. To his dismay and against his commands, awareness tightened his body below the belt.

"In the end," Annie continued, "you're going to choose a double Diablo burger with extra peppers, a side of sweet-potato fries—extra crispy, and a chocolate-banana shake."

Challenged, he leaned forward and met her glare. "How do you know what I want?"

"Because." She planted her palm down on the table

and leaned in till they were nearly nose to nose. "While you and your football buddies parked your cocky behinds in the booth by the door so all your minions could see you and come in to fawn all over you, some of us were slinging hash and cleaning up your mess after you left."

He leaned back. "I don't remember your working here."

"Why would you?" She shifted her weight again, and he'd have to be dead not to notice that somewhere between his last visit home and now, Annie had become quite a knockout. "In those days, you could barely see beyond Jessica Holt's big brown eyes and bodacious tatas. I, Annie of the flat-as-a-surfboard chest and metal mouth, deterred your hormonal-teenage-boy scrutiny."

She certainly wasn't flat-chested anymore.

He could argue about the hormonal part, but why bother. In high school, he'd been interested in three things; having fun, getting laid, and getting laid.

Some things were important enough to be counted twice.

"You make me sound like such a jackass."

One corner of her luscious pink lips kicked upward. "You were."

Yeah. He probably had been. And he wasn't really sure he appreciated the reminder.

"So why are you working here now?" he asked, deftly changing the subject. "Didn't you get enough slinging hash the first time around?"

"A girl's got to earn a living somehow. Slinging hash is all I've ever really done. My hand-dipped chocolates haven't exactly taken off like wildfire. And since Sweet's street corners are already occupied with whiskey barrels and petunias, there isn't any room for me to hang around waiting for customers."

"Always the smart-ass," he said.

"Takes one to know one."

Before he could protest, she lifted her hand off the table and stepped back with a serious look.

"When you're a single mom with a baby, you have to earn a living somewhere that will understand your child is your first priority. And that if they're sick, you might not be able to make it to work that day. Bud's a dad and a grandfather, so he understands. He also knows I'd never take his generosity for granted."

Shit. How could he have gotten so tangled up in his own troubles that he'd forgotten Annie was a single mom now after having been abandoned by her baby's slimeball father?

"How's Max doing?"

"Growing like the cutest weed in the garden of life." Pride burst across her pretty face. "He's walking now. Gets into everything. Izzy's trying to teach him to talk in sentences. But his favorite word is still *Mamamamamama*."

He chuckled, and the sensation that pushed through his chest felt as warm as sunshine. Then just as quick, regret that he'd missed so much kicked in. "It seems like I was gone for an eternity. I can't believe Max is walking. Reno and Charli have a baby. Jackson and Abby have one on the way. And Izzy's already started kindergarten."

"Your brother can't believe it either. I think it's hard for Jackson not seeing Izzy all the time because of the shared custody with Fiona. Even though Fiona's an amazing mom and they have such a wonderful relationship. Mostly he complains that Izzy's growing up so fast makes him feel old."

Jake got that. He felt ancient, and he'd just barely turned thirty-one. "So I guess you'll be at this get-together my mom is planning?"

"Wouldn't miss it for the world."

"I don't suppose you could talk her out of it."

Eyes wide, she exhaled a little puff of exasperation. "Are you kidding me?"

"Nope."

"Pardon me for being blunt, but why would you want to take that away from her?" She sighed, then glanced away when a customer called her name. With a nod in their direction, she brought her eyes back around to him, sharp and focused. "I know I can't imagine what you went through over there. And I know when you guys come back you don't always like to talk about it. But I was here with your mom when she got the call about what happened. I saw the absolute devastation and the fear on her face when she realized that not only had she lost her firstborn son and the husband she loved with all her heart, but that she'd also come very close to losing her baby boy. She's so damned happy you made it home, there's no way I'd try to talk her out of celebrating the fact that you're alive."

Rendered speechless for maybe the first time in his life, Jake lifted the glass of water to his mouth and sipped.

"You should be happy too, Jake."

With a thud, he set his glass down on the table. For a long, awkward, silent moment, he watched the condensation slide down the side of the glass pitted by many trips through the dishwasher. When he composed himself, he looked up and pushed the menu in her direction.

He wasn't happy.

And the constant ache in his chest made him realize he might never be happy again.

"So . . ." Annie tossed him a know-it-all glare. "Double Diablo burger with extra peppers, a side of sweet-potato fries—extra crispy, and a chocolate-banana shake?"

"Sure." Dammit. He hated to let her win.

One purple-polished fingernail dragged the menu across the table. Jake held his breath and willed her to leave. But, of course, this was Annie, and God knew the girl did things in her own damned way and in her own damned time.

"Well, even if *you* aren't happy . . ." She snatched up the menu. "*I'm* really glad you made it back."

SEEKING A MUCH-NEEDED break, Annie tossed Jake's menu on the stack of others near the cash register, gave Bud a finger-across-the-throat indication that she was momentarily frazzled, and headed toward the back door. The screen door slammed with a shotgun bang behind her as she leaned against the old yellow building and sucked in a calming lungful of warm air.

The relief of seeing Jake alive and back on home turf filled her heart with so much joy, it was hard to breathe.

The moment he'd walked through the door, she'd wanted to reach out and touch him to make sure he was real and not just another one of her highly imaginative dreams. But touching Jake had never been a part of her reality. And that's just one of the many things that sucked about worshipping from afar.

If she'd been a smoker, now would be the time she'd light one up to calm her nerves. Instead, she reached into the pocket of her apron, took out a watermelon-flavored Jolly Rancher, unwrapped it, and popped it into her mouth. The sugary tartness rolled over her tongue, and she closed her eyes to ward off the memories that nipped at her heels.

Closing her eyes only made those memories more powerful.

Why men had a habit of either rewriting history or dismissing it altogether, Annie didn't know. But it seemed Jake had fallen down the rabbit hole and forgotten how, once upon a time, they'd spent hours together having heart-to-heart discussions about everything from why girls spent so many hours in front of the mirror trying to perfect what God had given them to why guys had such a crazy need to be so rough-and-tumble. They'd discussed how difficult it had often been for him to keep up with his brothers when sometimes all he really wanted to do was go out and dig a garden or move some rocks to form a nice landscape. They'd talked about how she felt every time her parents left her and her sister alone to go party for days on end.

Back in the day, they'd been each other's confidants.

Then Jake had gone away to college and subsequently joined the Marines. And he'd forgotten about her. She couldn't help feeling a little lost after he'd walked out of her life. Sure, she'd had her sister to talk to. But Jake had been closer to her own age—only two years older— and he'd become the objective voice she'd needed when her demons tried to drag her down. Her personal testosterone-packed voice of reason.

She'd trusted him.

Completely.

When he was no longer there, she found, once again, she'd been left behind. Forgotten as though she didn't matter. Her response had been to make a string of really bad decisions.

Now it appeared Jake had forgotten—or dismissed— all those times they'd sat on a stack of hay bales in the barn, or ridden out over Wilder Ranch on horseback while they deliberated deep and sometimes dark matters of the heart. Now, it seemed like all he could remember about her was . . . well, nothing really. And that hurt. No matter how hard she tried not to let it.

Still, he was alive.

Thank God.

Beside her, the screen door creaked open, and a very pregnant Paige Marshall stepped out and joined her in the shade. For a moment, her friend and coworker said nothing, just rubbed her hands over her ever-increasing belly.

"Jake's hurting," Paige said with a little sigh. "I know because he's got that same haunted look in his eye that Aiden had when he came back from the war."

"Did he ever tell you what happened over there?"

"A little. Not all." Paige held out her hand. "Got another Jolly Rancher you can spare? This baby craves sweets, and I left my cinnamon bears at home."

Annie plopped an apple-flavored candy into Paige's hand and watched as her friend unwrapped it and stuck it in her mouth.

"Aiden thinks he's protecting me by not telling me," Paige explained. "But all he's really doing is trying to keep the pain from rising to the surface. Sometimes that makes things worse. But I guess until they're ready to tell the story, they'll continue to try to find a way to cope."

"Or realize they can't?" Annie asked.

"Yeah. But Jake has his brothers. They've all been in his shoes. They've all suffered in some way, shape, or form. They all lost their big brother. They know the pain. So, hopefully they'll, be able to get him to talk."

"What if he doesn't?"

Paige turned her shoulder to the wall and looked into Annie's face. "Then you'll be there to catch him when he falls."

"Me?" A cynical laugh pushed through Annie's lips as her heart stumbled. "I'd *never* be the one Jake would turn to if he needed someone. Not as a friend or anything else." At least not anymore.

"But you want to be?"

She blew out a sigh. "Guess there's no denying I've always had a crazy thing for him."

"Crazy as in he's so gorgeous you want to jump his bones? Or crazy as in you could see yourself spending the rest of your life with him?"

"Both. But he never really noticed me." In *that* way. Annie shook her head. "Still doesn't."

"Have you ever told him how you feel?"

Annie scoffed.

"That's a lot of time to be thinking about a man and never letting him know."

"Yep. A lonnnnng time." Annie sighed and rested the back of her head against the side of the building. "But for some reason, whenever I get around him, my emotions tangle up my words, and we end up arguing. So I never opened that door. At first I didn't because I didn't want him to laugh at me. Then . . ." She shrugged. "I don't know. I guess I just didn't ever want to hear him verify that he'd never feel the same about me."

"I totally get that. I told Aiden how I felt right after he came back, and he basically threw my words in my face."

"And yet, now you're married and have a baby on the way."

"Which wouldn't have happened if I'd let the stubborn and clueless man have his own way."

"I think about that. Jake almost died, and I never told him how I feel. Not that he'd care."

"Don't try to second-guess a Wilder, Annie. You won't win. And I'm willing to give Jake a lot more credit. He's a smart man."

"I know."

"Then why waste any more time? Why tempt fate?" Paige rubbed her hand over her belly again. "And just in case you were wondering, there's a remedy for that arguing thing you two frequently do."

"What's that? Duct-tape my mouth?"

After Paige quit laughing, she cupped her hands over Annie's shoulders. "No need for that. You just play it straight. Give him the business side of that mouth."

"Which is?"

"You just kiss the poor guy, Annie. If the words don't come out right, you let him know how you feel in a different way."

"That's what worked for Aiden?"

"That and a little moonlight."

"What if Jake's really *not* interested?"

"Then you get him to change his mind." Paige grinned. "You want proof that technique works? Look no further than your own sister. Abby was in love with Jackson forever. For years, he refused to move her out of the *friend* zone. And even though for a while they went their own ways, she finally found a way to sneak past that stubborn, locked-down heart of his." The hard candy clacked against Paige's teeth.

"And look at Charli," she continued. "Reno put up every barrier he could invent and then some to keep her away. But she still managed to get him to see reason. Although I suppose mentioning to him that she'd forgotten to put on panties while they were at the Wilder Barbecue Blowout might have helped a little."

They both giggled at that.

"And if you want to talk about accomplishing the impossible, look at Allison. She had the challenge of turning Sweet's most infamous playboy into a happily married man."

"I think it was the other way around with Allison and Jesse. Seems to me *he* was the one who had to do all the sweet-talking."

"An even better example of the endless possibilities." Paige gave Annie's shoulder a sympathetic pat. "Jake is a Wilder brother, Annie. He's not going to make it easy. But if you really do have strong feelings for him, I guarantee he'll be worth the trouble."

There had been a time in Annie's life when she'd have jumped through hoops, stuffed her bra with tissue, or learned the Victoria's Secret angels *slinky* walk to get Jake's attention. The fear of rejection and humiliation had always stopped her from going after what she'd wanted. Back in the day, he hadn't even put her in the friend zone, at least not when they'd been out in public. In private, he treated her completely different than he did in front of his family and friends. Those private moments they shared were few and far between. But they were precious. And she was pretty sure they meant a whole lot more to her than they ever did him.

Once he'd enlisted in the Marines, she knew he'd never come back and see her any different. He'd be too worldly. To him, she'd always be Annie Morgan, royal pain in the backside. She'd never be, Annie, the love of his life. So she'd moved on and away—almost two thousand miles—to try to find a life that would fill her soul with all the love and emotion she craved. Unfortunately, all she'd found was a low-paying job, loneliness, and heartache.

So much for grand ideas.

In Seattle, she thought she'd found love—her very

own Prince Charming. Doug had been a hot musician with plenty of edge to keep him interesting. His music had been reflective and romantic. He'd had dark curly hair and seductive eyes like Jim Morrison from The Doors.

It had taken her almost two long years after Doug had moved into her apartment to realize he'd been too focused on his career to pay her much mind. On the other hand, for him she'd been a passionate supporter of his music. A financial support so he could focus on his career. And doormat for him to wipe his feet on when he learned she was pregnant with his child.

Beneath Doug's stimulating rock-and-roll exterior, he hadn't been charming at all. What she'd really found beneath all that hair and songwriting genius was a toad who proved there was no room in his life for her or their child.

As Paige opened the screen door for them to go back inside the diner, Annie admitted she'd made plenty of mistakes in her life. Having her little boy wasn't one of them. But never letting Jake Wilder know how much she really cared might have been her most monumental.

Times had changed.

She was older, wiser, and she'd learned to never back down from what meant the most.

Jake meant something to her.

He always had.

He was far from perfect although he was perfect to look at. But she knew that deep down, beneath the shell of that gorgeous exterior; he was a man with heart, honor, and loyalty. He'd been raised to respect family and community. And she knew that just like his brothers, when he fell in love, he'd be a forever kind of guy.

The question now was . . . could he ever fall in love with *her*?

Maybe Paige was right. Maybe it was time to step up and find out. Wondering wouldn't ever give her an answer.

Determined, she smoothed her hands over her hair and down her skirt. At the window, she grabbed up Jake's order and headed toward his booth. As professionally as possible, she set his Diablo burger, fries, and milk shake in front of him. He looked up at her, eyes dark, blue, and intense.

"If there's anything else you want, anything at all, just let me know," she said. Then she gave him a "Brace yourself, cowboy" smile and walked away.

When she glanced back, he was still looking.

Indulge in the all of Candis
Terry's Sweet, Texas books!

Enter the World of Sweet, Texas!

Anything But Sweet

A Sweet, Texas Novel, Book 1

A man who doesn't like change . . .

For years, ex-Marine Reno Wilder managed
to uphold his end of the Wilder boys' wild
reputation. But the scars of war and the
deaths of those he loved have flipped the
switch on his point of view. Now, to keep
tradition and memories alive, he'll settle
for a staid life of wash, rinse, repeat.

When the senior citizens of Sweet, Texas,
believe it's time for their little town to
become a destination for tourists, they
contact a new TV makeover show. Their
community is chosen to participate and
everyone is pleased—except Reno.

A woman who wants to change everything . . .

Beneath her headstrong desire to upend
Reno's peace and quiet, makeover show
host and designer Charlotte Brooks has
something to offer that has nothing to
do with changing drapes and everything
to do with showing him that change can
be sexy, hot, and very, very sweet.

Faceoff for a happily-ever-after . . .

Neither of them saw coming. Who will
stand their ground? Who will find common
ground? And who will let go of their past
and grab hold of a future full of promise?

Sweetest Mistake

A Sweet, Texas Novel, Book 2

From the moment he became her toddler-
sized sandbox-knight-in-shining-armor to
the day he went off to war, Jackson Wilder has
secretly been in love with Abigail Morgan.
She's his best friend and the first girl he
ever made love to. With the sands of war
at the bottom of his hourglass, he heads
home to surprise Abby and finally profess
his love. But as everyone knows, surprises
can backfire, and upon his return, Jackson
discovers that his news comes way too late.

Abby has made some mistakes in her life
but none as monumental as marrying a man
she barely knew and sinking into a loveless
marriage. When she hits the age of thirty, her
job as a trophy wife comes to an abrupt end, and
there's no place for her to go but home. Abby
thinks she's learned her lesson the hard way
until she returns to Sweet. And a homecoming
just wouldn't be complete without coming face-
to-face with her biggest—and sexiest—mistake.

Home Sweet Home

A Sweet, Texas Novella

**Before Candis Terry's wild Wilder
brothers met their matches, a soldier
gets a homecoming in Sweet, Texas**

HE'S GIVEN UP . . .

Army Ranger, Lieutenant Aiden Marshall,
fought in some of the most hellish corners
on earth and survived. Those closest to him,
did not. When he returns home to Sweet,
Texas, he believes he's broken and has lost
everything—including his soul. The only
fair thing he can do is tell the woman who's
patiently waited for him to come home—to
move on with her life—without him.

. . . BUT SHE NEVER WILL

Sassy waitress Paige Walker has no intention
of walking away from the man of her dreams.
He gave his all for his country and served with
honor. Now it's time to pull him from the
darkness and give him hope. With a heap of

love, the help of the entire town, and a tail-wagging companion, Paige makes sure her hero knows there's no place like home sweet home.

Something Sweeter

A Sweet, Texas Novel, Book 3

A dream come true . . .

To the single women of Sweet, Texas, former
Marine, Jesse Wilder, is hot, hunky perfection
with six-pack abs and a heart of gold. He's
a veterinarian who loves animals, kids, is
devoted to his family, and is financially stable.

The best part? No woman has yet snagged
him or put a ring on his finger.

The problem? Jesse's been down a long, bumpy
road and isn't the least bit interested in
setting his boots on the path to matrimony.

Comes heart to heart with a wedding
planner and her big secret . . .

Sure, Allison Lane makes a living helping
others plan their big day, but that doesn't mean
she has to actually believe in matrimonial bliss.
Her family's broken track record proves she just
doesn't have the settle-down gene swimming in
her DNA. And though she finds Jesse fantasy

material, why should she take the word of this confirmed playboy that all roads lead to "I do?"

In their battle for a happily-ever-after.

Sweet Fortune

A Sweet, Texas Novella

Sarah Randall has lost her job, her apartment, and her patience hoping for her own Mr. Right. Tired of being invisible to the opposite sex, a leap of faith sends her straight to Sweet, Texas. There she encounters sexy Deputy Brady Bennett. To catch his eye, Sarah needs to face her fears and become a woman interesting enough to pique his curiosity.

Deputy Brady Bennett thought he had his life all tied up in a pretty package, but she married someone else. Determined not to suffer another heartbreak, he finds he can't resist the fascination attached to the gifts that mysteriously turn up in his mailbox. Will his secret admirer ever reveal herself? And if she does, will he be ready to let love in?

Sweet Cowboy Christmas

A Sweet, Texas Novella

Mistletoe, holly, and cowboys, oh my!
Christmas in Texas has never been sweeter.

Years ago, Chase Morgan traded in his
dusty cowboy boots for the shimmering
lights of New York City and a fast track
up the corporate ladder. But when his
shiny life is turned on end just in time
for Christmas, Chase knows he needs to
reevaluate even if that means going home to
Texas to endure his least favorite holiday.

When Mr. Tall, Dark, and Smoking Hot
walks through her door at the Magic Box
Guest Ranch, Faith Walker sees just another
handsome, rich exec looking to play cowboy
for a week at her expense. She's sure the
grumpy, but sexy as hell Scrooge will put a
crimp in her holly jolly plans. Until a sizzling
kiss has her seeing him in a new light.

Chase is haunted by secrets, and even though
it goes entirely against her "hands off the
guests" rule, Faith is tempted to help him leave

the past behind. As the magic of the season
swirls around them, she is determined to
succeed because now she is certain one sweet,
cowboy Christmas will never be enough.

Sweet Surprise

A Sweet, Texas Novel, Book 4

Fiona Wilder knows all about falling in lust. Love? That's another story. Determined not to repeat past mistakes, the single mom and cupcake shop owner is focused on walking the straight and narrow. But trouble has a way of finding her. And this time it comes in the form of a smoking hot firefighter who knows all the delicious ways to ignite her bad girl fuse.

Firefighter Mike Halsey learned long ago that playing with fire just gets you burned. He's put his demons behind him, and if there's one line he won't cross, it's getting involved with his best friend's ex. But when fate throws him in the path of the beautiful, strong, and off-limits Fiona, will he be able to fight their attraction? Or will he willingly go down in flames?

Truly Sweet

A Sweet Texas Novel, Book 5

When the one you've always wanted . . .

At sixteen, Annabelle Morgan hoped her crush on Jake Wilder was just a passing phase. Now she's twenty-nine, and nothing has changed—except Jake. The once-carefree Marine has come home with a giant chip on his shoulder. He insists a single mom like Annie deserves more than he can offer. Yet no matter how gruff his gorgeous exterior may be, Jake's toe-curling kisses convince her that this attraction is definitely mutual.

Becomes the one who wants you back . . .

Butting heads with feisty Annie was always a thrill. Add other body parts to the mix, and Jake is in serious trouble. He can't be a forever-and-family guy—and Annie's not a friends-with-benefits kind of woman. But love has a way of changing the best-laid plans, and surrender has never been so tempting . . .

The outcome is truly sweet.

About the Author

CANDIS TERRY was born and raised near the sunny beaches of Southern California and now makes her home on an Idaho farm. She's experienced life in such diverse ways as working in a Hollywood recording studio to chasing down wayward steers. Only one thing has remained the same: her passion for writing stories about relationships, the push and pull in the search for love, and the security one finds in their own happily-ever-after.

Discover great authors, exclusive offers, and more at hc.com.